THE LIAR'S WIFE

KIERSTEN MODGLIN

www.kierstenmodglinauthor.com
Cover Design: Tadpole Designs
Editing: Three Owls Editing
Proofreading: My Brother's Editor
Formatting: Tadpole Designs
First Print Edition: 2020
First Electronic Edition: 2020

To my aunts, Lori and Velma, for cheering me on with each book and always asking about the next.

"Just because something isn't a lie does not mean that it isn't deceptive. A liar knows that he is a liar, but one who speaks mere portions of truth in order to deceive is a craftsman of destruction."

CRISS JAMI

CHAPTER ONE

When my eyes opened, there was only darkness. Darkness like I'd never seen before, with not a hint of light anywhere. A clump of something heavy and moist sat in my mouth.

Panic.

What was happening?

Ice-cold fear flooded through my veins at lightning speed.

Where was I? What had happened? I tried to sit up, tried to shove myself free, but I couldn't move. I was frozen in place, kept there by some invisible force. It was heavy and thick, a texture I didn't recognize at first. I'd been placed inside of something. Under something. I couldn't tell.

I inhaled, and the thick clump moved further down my throat. I couldn't breathe. My body flailed and convulsed, trying to free itself as my mind went to a flash of bright light.

Was I going to die right then and there? In some

unrecognizable place? Alone and cold? There didn't seem to be any other options.

I panicked, trying to cough and struggle against the force holding me down. *What is happening? What is happening? What is happening?* I fought through the cobwebs of my nightmare-filled memory.

Finally, my hand wriggled free, moving through something thick and unrelenting to touch my face. At first it didn't register what was happening. Where I was. How I'd gotten there. What I needed to do. Then, all at once, realization slammed into my chest. I realized where I was and what was happening. I knew who had put me there.

I knew I was going to die.

With as much force as I could muster, I shoved my hands upward, roaring through the mud in my mouth and throat. I fought through a thick layer of the moist, wet earth, and then my hands were free. Like a zombie from the grave, my hands tore through the earth to reach the fresh air above. Was my assailant still there?

I didn't care. Couldn't. I was free. I felt the cool night air on my skin as I pushed myself to sit up, coughing and spewing mucus-covered soil from my mouth.

I looked around me at the fresh dirt that was meant to be my grave. The night air was cool, and there were no stars in the sky. No light to be seen, and yet, still somehow the air was lighter than being underground. I stood up, dusting myself off. The dirt was caked into my teeth, my nails, my clothes, my hair. I was walking proof monsters existed. If I came upon me in the woods, I'd run.

I spit again, trying to free my mouth of the sour,

bloody taste of the dirt, and brush the mud from my hair. Where was I? Which direction should I go?

I had no idea. No idea about any of it. No idea how I got there or where *there* was. I reached up and touched my scalp, then jerked my hand back in agonizing pain. When I pulled my hand away, warm, sticky blood coated my palm. Though I couldn't see it clearly in the darkness, I knew what it was. I put my fingers to my scalp again, feeling the open wound just above my temple. A piece of skin hung over, so loose I could've pulled it off if it didn't sting so badly.

I tried to take a step forward, but pain tore through my body, my nerves on high alert. *What happened to me?*

I ran my hands along my body, down my thigh, and realized it was just as painful, just as wet with blood, but from a different wound. I hobbled forward, brushing dirt from my eyes and mouth with every painful step. It hurt. It all burned and throbbed and ached. Every part of me. I couldn't seem to remember anything, my mind a dark, foggy mess of fuzzy memories. What was real and what wasn't? What had I done? What had led me to an early, yet ultimately ineffective grave?

Who tried to kill me?

The last thing I remembered was...*her.* I remembered the fight. I remembered learning about her. I remembered confronting her. Remembered it all coming together for me at once. I remembered the pain.

Pain.

Physical and emotional. All of it. At the thought, lightning-sharp pain shot through me, and I hobbled and cried and gasped for air as my lungs worked to free the mud from my sticky throat. I bent over, my body rigid with pain and trepidation as I coughed then winced, coughed then winced.

I tasted blood then, and I wondered if it was coming from my head or somewhere else entirely. How else had I been hurt? What had I been through? It was coming back to me slowly, as if I were scraping mud from the memories right along with the rest of my body.

The forest was dense with trees, so thick and so dark, they were all I could make out in the distance. Trees, branches, shadows. The woods were quiet all around me, but as I made it a bit farther, I saw the first sign of light. The moon lit up the night sky above me, giving me glimpses of the forest around me.

The trees were thick, the earth foggy, and my head painful. So, so much pain. I couldn't think straight, couldn't move. I should've looked over the gravesite closer for an explanation as to how I got there, but I had no way to see it and no desire to go back. Whoever put me there obviously believed I was dead, and I knew who it was. *Her.*

She'd had enough of me getting in her way and decided to end it, but she wasn't going to do away with me so easily. I wasn't going down without a fight.

I saw the road then, up ahead, and I forced myself forward. Each step was agonizing, each breath like a scalding dagger to the stomach. I stepped down into the ditch and out of the woods, and then back up the embankment and toward the road. *I must look like a nightmare; who would ever stop for me?*

To my surprise, someone did. The dark truck pulled to

a stop next to me, and the man in the driver's seat leaned over as he rolled the window down, taking in my appearance. He was old, haggard, worn. The truck smelled of cigarettes and chewing tobacco.

"Do you need some help?" he asked. Question of the century. I obviously had a genius on my hands.

"Yes. Please."

He reached over further, pushing the door open. He wasn't afraid of me. Even bloody and covered in dirt, I didn't appear to be a threat. It must be why I went down so easily. But I felt like I'd been reborn, and I wouldn't be so easy to take down the next time.

I was coming for what was mine.

I climbed into the truck, the pain of each movement unrelenting. It hurt. It all just…hurt.

He pulled out a cell phone. "Do you want me to call an ambulance? The police?" He swallowed as he stared at me, apparently more afraid now.

"Thank you, but I'll be okay. Can you just take me home?" I asked. My voice was gravelly and unfamiliar. How long had it been since I used it?

I would be okay, just as soon as I ended this once and for all. I couldn't do that if the police were involved.

He nodded, his hands shaking as he moved to put the car into drive. "What happened to you?"

I didn't answer him because I didn't know. I stared out the window, my body roaring with agony, and all I could think of was how I let myself get here. How I let her ruin my life.

CHAPTER TWO

TWO AND A HALF WEEKS EARLIER

"Careful," I warned in a whisper as Ben pushed open the door to our home.

He nodded at me, a smile growing on his face as he continued forward, careful not to bump the car seat and its precious cargo as we stepped across the threshold. I was sore in so many ways, the scar on my lower stomach still ached like it might split open whenever I coughed or laughed or sneezed, but I ached in a different way, too… for the baby just a few feet away from me. I hated being separated from him for any length of time. I'd never thought I could be so attached to anyone.

He rested the car seat on the coffee table, setting the brand new diaper bag beside it. Inside the seat, Gray was still sleeping peacefully. He didn't know that when he opened his eyes, the world he thought he knew, the one that consisted only of the small three-hundred-square-foot hospital room, would be so much bigger and more different than he could've imagined. The only thing familiar now would be the two of us. The two people who loved him most in the world.

Ben held out a hand. "Want me to take that?" He gestured toward the overnight bag thrown over my shoulder. I handed it to him, thankful for the relief from carrying it. Even though it wasn't nearly over the ten-pound weight limit my doctor had recommended, every ounce of added strain on my muscles was torture. "Leave the pain medicine out on the counter," I reminded him as he made his way into the kitchen. He nodded and began searching the bag, leaving Gray and me alone.

I eased down on the couch, clenching my pelvis as I felt a gush of blood. *Don't leak, don't leak, don't leak.* I stood back up, pulling one of the disposable bed pads the nurse gave me from the diaper bag and laying it down on the edge of the couch. I sank back down, thankful for the extra protection, then looked over at my son.

The word still felt foreign to me.

Son.

I had a son.

I was a mom.

How strange…and yet, how wonderful. I reached my hand forward, pressing a finger to one of his tiny feet. I needed to touch him as much as I needed to breathe. It was instinctual. I wondered how mad Ben would be if I took him from the car seat. It was sure to wake him up, but I just wanted him close to me. Closer than he already was. I teared up at the mere thought of him, *damn baby blues.* Ben was busy with the bag, not paying attention as I moved toward our son.

I unbuckled him, lifting his tiny hands away from the straps one at a time as I removed them. He stirred, his little lips opening, and a tiny mitten-clad fist moved to rub his eyes.

"Hey there, Gray baby," I whispered, lifting him from the seat and resting him on my chest. I leaned back on the couch, heaving a sigh of relief as his breathing seemed to slow mine. Just two days ago, he was still a part of me. Still inside my body. How was it possible he was on his own already? That I was back on mine?

"Did he wake up?" Ben asked, zipping back across the room as Gray let out a soft coo.

"No, he's back asleep," I told him quietly, feeling my breasts swelling with milk as his body heat warmed my skin. "I just wanted to hold him."

Ben lifted the seat and placed it on the floor, coming to sit down beside me. His finger traced Gray's cheek. "He's incredible," he whispered, and I felt tears collecting in my eyes again.

"I don't ever want to let him go."

He put a hand on my back, graciously ignoring my tears as he'd had to for the past two days. No one told me being a new mom would turn me into a crier.

He slid his hand up my back, gripping my shoulder lovingly. "Do you want to get some rest? The doctor said you should sleep while he does."

Even though I hadn't slept much at all over the past two days, I didn't feel the least bit tired. I didn't want to put Gray down, but when I shook my head, he began to stir, negating the offer. His head lifted and bobbed away from my chest as he searched for a food source.

I scooted back on the couch, placing the pillow under my arm and obliging. "There you go, Gray baby," I whispered, my voice low and soothing, though I was in pain again. My stomach cramped, and I felt a new gush of blood between my legs as he suckled at my breast. Ben stood at once, grabbing his Boppy pillow and wrapping it around my waist. He bent down, pulling my shoes from my feet and moving the coffee table toward me so my feet could rest there. He walked back across the room and into the kitchen, and returned a moment later with a glass of water, one slice of lemon in it.

"Here you go." He placed the straw next to my mouth and I took a sip, then he reached across me, careful of Gray's head, and put the glass on my table.

"Thank you, baby," I said, my eyes already trained on my son once again.

"Well, what do you think? You want to keep him?" Ben joked, wrapping an arm around me to peer down at him.

I wrinkled my nose. "He's absolutely perfect, Ben," I said, cuddling Gray closer to me as his eyes rolled back with delight, white milk bubbles forming at the corner of his mouth. My eyes felt heavy suddenly, as if I could've fallen asleep at any moment, and I wondered how I'd felt so awake just moments before.

As Gray fell away from my chest, I felt Ben reach for him. He kissed my cheek as he took the baby from my arms. I smiled at him, my body burning warm and light with sleep as he pulled the blanket from the back of the couch with one arm and used it to cover me.

"I'm so tired," I whispered, though he must've known it.

"I know, baby. Go to sleep. Daddy'll take over for a while." He cuddled Gray into his chest, bouncing him softly.

"He'll need to be burped," I reminded him as I stifled a yawn.

Ben began patting his back, whispering softly in his ear as Gray fussed.

"It's okay, little guy. Daddy's here." He winked at me as I closed my eyes a final time. Everything in me wanted to be awake, be present to see all the changes, every moment that I knew I'd miss while I slept, but I couldn't. I couldn't fight sleep for a second longer.

Darkness found me, and I drifted off to sleep to the sound of Ben humming a song I couldn't recall the name of.

CHAPTER THREE

I rocked Gray carefully, humming in his ear long past the time he'd fallen asleep. I couldn't get over how much I loved feeling his little chest rise and fall against mine.

I could've lain there all day. No place to go. Nothing to do. I could've lain still and held my child until he outgrew my arms. I glanced at the clock as a familiar dull ache grew in my lower stomach. It was past the time for me to take my medicine, but Ben had been in the bathroom for quite a while.

I sat still, trying to think of something else. He'd be out soon. I could wait. When a second wave of achiness came on a few minutes later, I winced, shifting my weight carefully. I lifted Gray away from me and laid him down, careful to keep his face away from the back of the couch. I patted his tummy as he tightened his arms and legs, aware of my absence, but quickly calmed down.

I grasped my own stomach as I moved to stand,

putting pressure on my scar to keep the pain at bay. I moved slowly across the apartment, every move met with a bolt of pain. When I reached the counter, I picked up the bottle and twisted it open, taking my pill without water.

I couldn't hear the shower still running from the bathroom. *What is he up to?* "Ben?" I whisper-yelled, praying I wouldn't need to walk that far. The nurses had told me not to miss a dose; it was harder to get back out of pain once you were in it, and better to stay on top of it. Until that moment, we'd been incredibly diligent with my regimen.

When he didn't answer, I sucked in a shallow breath and pushed off from the counter, easing my way down the hall, my hands on both sides to keep me from falling.

I made it to the bedroom door and pushed it open carefully. His back was to the door, already fully dressed, though his hair was wet.

"Aww, well, thank you," he said, both hands cradling the phone.

I stepped in further, my brows drawn down. He spun in a circle slowly, pacing the floor, and when his eyes met mine, his expression grew serious.

"Hey, listen, I've got to go," he said, lowering his phone without warning.

"Who were you talking to?" I asked, my voice powerless. The look on his face—the shame, the denial, it was all too familiar.

"Sorry. Just Jason, from the hardware store. He called to wish us congratulations."

"Why were you hiding out in here?" I asked, cocking my head to the side.

He shoved the phone into his pocket with a scoff. "I wasn't *hiding out.* I didn't want to wake Gray. Was I being too loud?"

I shook my head. "No, I was just worried about you. I couldn't hear the shower anymore."

He grabbed a comb from the top of his dresser and ran it through his hair. "You shouldn't be worried about me, sweetheart. You should be on the couch, resting." He placed the comb back down and slid an arm under mine. "Let me help you. It should be about time for your medicine, isn't it?"

I winced as he pulled us forward, then he realized he was moving too fast and slowed down. "Sorry."

"I already took it," I told him, not bothering to mention it was late.

"I'm sorry it took me so long," he said, helping me to sit down once we arrived at the couch. "Do you want some lunch?"

I nodded halfheartedly, my mind still on the phone call. "I didn't know you and Jason were close." He pulled the table closer to me so I could prop up my swollen feet and walked into the kitchen, glancing back.

"Huh? Oh, we're not. I think he was hoping I'd say I was coming back to work, honestly. They're short-staffed. I didn't take the bait." He didn't look me in the eye as he said it—too busy digging through drawers—and eventually pulled out the cutting board.

"Well, it was nice of him to call, anyway."

"Mhm," he said, opening the fridge. I couldn't help wondering what he was hiding and whether or not I was overreacting. Ben had never been one to hide things from me. He knew about my history with Nate, but now I had the inclination that he was hiding his phone calls, and though I tried to brush it off, the tiniest voice in my head was screaming the loudest.

Something is not right.

CHAPTER FOUR

"Just make sure to warm the milk before you feed him, but test it on your wrist to be sure it's not too hot. And you may have to work with him. He was resisting the bottle a bit yesterday." I paced the apartment, checking to be sure I had everything, though I'd laid it all out the day before. *Pump, lunch, purse.* I was trying to stay busy to keep from crying. That was my only goal.

"I've got it, babe," Ben said. He rested an elbow on the countertop, cradling Gray in his arms. "I promise you we'll be fine. And you'll be home before you know it."

I spun away from him, pretending to search the fridge for something as I squeezed my eyes shut. He was just two days shy of two weeks old. I'd had such a short time getting to enjoy him, but my client list was backing up. For the sake of my sanity, I couldn't afford to miss any more work.

"I know you'll be fine," I said, spinning back around and walking toward them. I stroked Gray's cheeks, leaning in and pressing my lips to his scalp. I inhaled the scent of him, wanting every note ingrained into my memory. "I'm sorry. I'm just nervous."

"Do you want to hold him again before you go?" Ben asked, lifting Gray's body toward me.

I held a hand up. "No. If I do," my throat grew tight as fresh tears stung my eyes, "I'll just cry." It was too late. I already was.

Ben's eyes grew sad, and he cocked his head to the side. "You don't have to start back today, Palmer. Just take another week off."

"It won't be any easier then, either," I said. "It's like a bandage, right? Rip it off." I wiped a tear away and stalked past him, lifting my bags. "I'll have my phone with me, so if you need anything, just call. I have two meetings this afternoon, so I don't know how much I'll be able to text you, but if you call, I'll pick up or call you right back. I should be home around five."

Ben nodded, swaying in place with Gray as he began to fuss. He needed me. He wanted me. I was walking away.

I was so incredibly jealous of my husband. From the moment we found out we were expecting, I knew he'd be the one to stay home. I made three times what he did. He wouldn't make enough to cover childcare. I carried the health insurance, his company didn't have it. I enjoyed my job, he didn't.

There were so many reasons that this was the most logical choice, but that didn't mean I wasn't feeling resentful at that moment. He was content, still dressed in pajamas, cradling the baby, while I was shoved into work clothes, still bleeding and sore, with swollen breasts and baggy eyes, trying to pretend to be the woman I was not even two weeks ago when everything in my life had changed.

I opened the front door, trying to keep my voice steady as fresh tears flooded my vision, ruining whatever makeup I'd attempted to apply. "I love you both."

"We love you, too, Mama," Ben said, waving Gray's tiny hand. I sniffled, hugging them both again. At my touch, Gray began wailing, his mouth opening and closing like a fish waiting to be fed. "I've got him," Ben promised, lifting Gray to his chest. "I've got you, don't I, big guy?" He walked toward the kitchen, and I stood still, inadequate in every way. Already late for work and unable to feed my child. I was failing at everything.

I turned, stepping through the door and slamming it shut. My back rested against the wood of it as I gave in to the sobs that were so tight in my chest.

I walked down the steps, crying and snotting, one minute feeling like I could pull it together and the next desperate to turn around and run back to my child. None of what I was doing felt natural. Had we made a mistake? Should I have asked Ben to find something better? Given up a job that I love? I wanted to put Gray back in my belly. Take him with me wherever I went again like I had for nine months.

I stepped outside of our apartment building and hurried to my car across the street with blurring vision. Once I was in, I pulled the visor down, looking myself over, cleaning up my makeup, and turning on the radio. It would all be okay. I just had to make it through the next eight hours. After that, I'd be back home. I'd see him again.

I put the car in drive, hating everything about the way I felt as I drove farther and farther away from my whole world.

Thirty minutes later, I was walking into the office, my makeup fixed, hair fluffed, and fresh lipstick applied. I wished no one would ask about him. If I didn't think about it, maybe it would hurt less.

I rode the elevator to the fifth floor with a man who talked loudly on his cell phone the whole way, thankful not to have to make small talk. When I stepped off the elevator and into the office, the familiar, clean scent hit me and put me at ease.

"Palmer!" Howie, my sweetheart of an assistant, called, waving as he stood from his desk. He rushed forward, holding his hands out. "Welcome back! Need me to take anything?"

I shook my head, holding tightly to my bags. "I've got them. Thanks, Howie."

"I can't wait to see more pictures of the little guy. He's so adorable!" He smiled, his grin wide and full of excitement as he walked with me toward my office.

"Thanks," I said, surprised that I didn't feel as sad as I'd expected to.

"Welcome back, Palmer!" Dannika said, waving at me from her office as she hung up the phone. She stood, too, rushing over and pulling me into a hug.

"Hey, love," I said as Howie pushed open my office door. I placed the bags on my desk, looking around the office I'd meticulously decorated. There was an ultrasound photograph in the far corner that I couldn't wait to replace with new pictures of Gray.

"How are you?" Dannika asked, resting a fist on her hip.

I smiled, trying to fake it, but my expression must've given me away. She leaned in, wrapping her arms around my neck and rubbing my back. I blinked heavily, trying to fight back the tears. As they began to fall, Howie joined our hug, both of them holding my weight as I felt like I could collapse.

We stayed like that for so long, I'd almost forgotten where we were. After a while, I pulled away, wiping my eyes. Dannika grabbed a tissue from the desk and passed it over. She rested against the table in the corner of the office. "It's hard," she said, her voice full of understanding. "I know, girl. I thought we were going to have to become homeless after I had Darius. I would've lived out of a box if it meant I could be home with that baby for a few more weeks."

Howie nodded. "That's why Dan started GloTech. When we adopted Gracie, we knew one of us would want to be home. I know it doesn't feel like it, but you're so lucky that Ben was able to stay home with him."

"You're right," I told him. And he was. "I know. It's just…so hard."

"It gets easier, but it's hard, girl. You're back entirely too early, too. I can't even imagine. I took the full twelve weeks off, and it still about killed me," Dannika said, crossing her arms.

"I need to work," I said. "Two weeks with no pay and a

mountain of hospital debt from his birth isn't going to cut it."

"Six-billion-dollar company and we can't even afford *paid maternity leave*," Dannika said, raising her voice so it carried across the quiet office. "Absolute trash, if you ask me." She rolled her eyes. "What can we do for you?"

"Anything," Howie offered. "Coffee, ice cream, distractions..."

"Distractions," I told him. "And lots of them. What have I missed?"

"Cumberland has a new assistant—"

"Kimberly," Howie and Dannika said in a nasally, drawn-out voice at the same time.

"Bright as a burned-out light bulb, that one," Dannika said.

"She's the worst," Howie agreed. "You'll see."

Dannika held her hands out in front of her breasts. "Cumberland likes what she brings to the table."

I snorted. "Anything client-wise? How did the King wedding go?"

"Magical," Dannika said, waving her hands in front of her face. "And they were great about you not being there. In fact, they sent you a card to wish you congratulations." She pointed to my desk. "I slid it in the top drawer."

I moved behind the desk and turned my keys in the lock, pulling it open to reveal a pink envelope. I opened it, watching as a gift card fell out. "They're so great," I said, my eyes watering again.

"*You're* so great, Palmer. You put in eighty hours on that wedding, *double* what they paid you for, and you threw together a goat-yoga-reception, *whatever the hell that is,* when the bride saw one and just had to have it at the last minute. You were a rock star, and you deserve all the credit."

"Thanks, Dannika." I couldn't help smiling. Despite how badly I didn't want to be there, Dannika and Howie were the only people who kept me sane most days. Dannika and I were partners. We'd climbed the company ladder together, and I'd hired Howie three years ago, the perfect addition to our group. I wasn't sure what I'd do without these two.

Howie's eyes lit up. "Oh! And, we forgot to tell you, the client you're meeting this afternoon is—"

"No, make her guess it!" Dannika said, holding her hand out.

"Guess it? Oh, gosh, I don't know!" I said, waiting.

"Guess!" Dannika demanded. "Dream client, *dream* budget, dream job."

"Dream*y* client," Howie said, wiggling his eyebrows playfully.

I giggled at the two of them, obviously pleased with themselves. "Is it someone I've worked with before?"

"Never. New client for the company, and he asked for you specifically," Dannika said, pointing to me.

I sank down in my chair, moving my bags to the floor. "Who is it? Tell me!"

"Grant Anderson!" Howie cried, practically jumping for joy.

"What?"

"He said Grant Anderson, baby," Dannika shouted with a gleeful cry, arms in the air. "Top forty, under forty, CEO of three out of four of Oceanside's leading startups, filthy rich, devilishly handsome, and he wants you to plan Anderson Enterprises' third anniversary party. There's an email in your inbox, but I believe his exact words were…"

She looked at Howie, who finished the sentence for her, his arms out to his sides. "Spare no expense!"

"You guys are kidding. Come on, it's not funny to tease a new mom," I said, already moving my mouse to start up the computer.

"Honest to God," Dannika said, hands up to show her innocence.

"Why me?" There were two hundred eighty-three unread emails in my inbox. I began to scroll.

"Well, as the CEO of the *other* leading Oceanside startup, Dan may have dropped a few hints that he was planning to have you plan his anniversary party at a fundraising event Anderson attended. Anderson's always looking to one-up GloTech. Two days later, we got the call."

"Oh my gosh, I could kiss him!" I cry as I finally reach the email. "Ben and I are taking you two out for a nice dinner, you know that?"

Howie beamed. "Oh, no need…but if you insist, we'll have steak." He winked. "Anyway, Anderson's super excited to work with you, and Cumberland is, of course, thrilled that we got the deal. If you can pull this off, you'll be Cumberland royalty."

"She already is," Dannika said. "That's why she gets the best clients." She lowered her voice. "After this deal, we'll finally have enough to break away and start our own company. And the clients he sends will be coming *your* way, not Cumberland's."

I swallowed. It was something we'd talked about since we graduated, but it still seemed too unrealistic. Especially now, with a baby. Insurance alone would keep me working there for much longer than I liked to think about. "Maybe," I said.

"Come on, babe. We've got this." Dannika tapped the frame on my desk, where my favorite quote sat.

If you don't take risks, you'll always work for someone who does. -Nora Denzel

With three kids, but a lawyer for a husband, Dannika's risks weren't exactly the same as mine. If she knew I'd had my share of our startup in savings for over a year now, she'd be so upset, but I couldn't bring myself to tell her. The risks still terrified me. As brave as I wanted to be, my comfort zone wasn't such a bad place to be.

Before I could respond, I watched as Mr. Cumberland appeared in my doorway. "Palmer, welcome back. We've missed you."

"Yeah, you're such a hero, Palmer. Coming back to work *less than two weeks* after having a human literally exit your body," Howie said, enunciating the words. "Even before your doctor cleared you."

Mr. Cumberland nodded enthusiastically, not realizing—or caring—the comments were sarcastic. "Palmer's a fighter, always has been."

Dannika rolled her eyes, not bothering to hide her irritation. "It would really be a shame if she were able to take more time off, wouldn't it?"

"Why on earth would she want to do that?" he asked. "Did they already tell you about your client meeting today? Big deal!" His fingers rubbed together, gesturing that I'd make a lot of money, ergo, *he'd* make a lot of money.

"They mentioned Grant Anderson, yes," I said, smiling politely. I didn't have enough energy to hate the man standing in front of me. Not for being unwilling to give me paid time off, not for not even mentioning Gray, not even for expecting me to jump straight into work. I just didn't have it in me.

Dannika's brows shot up, and I knew she wanted me to admit she was right. If we had our own business, I could work from home when I needed to. She could've taken on the extra clients to give me the time off with Gray.

Someday...

Mr. Cumberland sat down in front of my desk. "I needed to talk to you two about the month's numbers, anyway. Howie, can you send Ethan in?"

"Sure thing," Howie said, stepping back from the office at his apparent dismissal.

Already, we were in a business meeting.

Welcome back.

"WELL, I can certainly look into the ice sculpture of your logo. We hire a company in Oceanside that handles them. You'll love their work. We could even have them do the Anderson Enterprises name and then the logo below, if you'd like. I can have them draft up a few options for you to choose from."

Grant Anderson nodded, his eyes trained on his

phone. He wasn't really listening and kept having to have me repeat things.

"Does that work?"

"Yes, yes, definitely. Just have them send them over."

"Okay, great," I said, letting out a sigh. It was just after three, and my breasts were swollen with milk. I needed to pump desperately, but our meeting had run longer than expected. "So, then we just need to go over a catering list and I think we have all the basics."

"I've already chosen everything I'd like served. It's in the packet there," he said, waving his hand toward me. "Now, do you hire the wait staff?"

"Yes, like I mentioned before, we'll take care of handling—"

"One moment—"

He held up a hand, answering his phone. "Hello?"

I jerked my head back in shock. He couldn't be serious.

"Hey, no, sorry, I was in the middle of something. What's the status?" He paused. "No kidding? Yeah, we should. Call that girl from the other night, too…what was her name?" Another pause. "No, the one from Cincinnati. Yes, that's the one." Again, another pause. "We'll take the jet."

I tapped my fingers on the tabletop in the conference room, my breasts so tight, itchy, and uncomfortable, I knew I was going to be leaking any moment. It was the third phone call he'd answered in our two-hour-long meeting, where we'd only covered half of what we needed to, despite only being scheduled for an hour.

This client is important.

This client could change my life.

This client is infuriating.

"Oh my God, you didn't? Okay, yeah, you have to tell me what happened." He paused, letting out a laugh. "I would've died."

Anger radiated through me and, finally, I could take no more. I stood from the table, shoving my chair back. I grabbed my things.

"Hey—hey—ho—hold up. Hang on." He put his fingers over the speaker. "It'll just be a minute," he promised, already returning to his conversation. "Sorry, man."

"No, it won't be a minute," I said, shaking my head. His attention was pulled back to me.

"Excuse me?"

"You had me booked for an hour, and it's now been two." I glanced at my watch, though I knew I was correct. "I'm one of the most sought-after event planners in the South, Mr. Anderson, as you well know. If you have no time for this meeting, I'll ask that you reschedule. I, for one, don't have time to sit here any longer. You've wasted enough of my time." I lifted my folders to my chest to cover my light-colored blazer as his eyes fell to my chest.

He put the phone down, looking shocked. "I don't think you realize how big of a deal this party could be for your company, Ms. Lewis. I'd think that running a little long would be worth it for you."

"Well—" I dug in my heels. Cumberland was going to kill me. "You thought wrong. You may find planners who will sit and let you walk all over them, but I am not one of those. My time is valuable, Mr. Anderson, and I have other clients to attend to. Losing your business will not be the end of the world for me, but losing my time and attention may well hurt your party. I am the best in the business, which means I don't have to sit around and get treated like this. I'm sure you're very used to being able to treat people how you please, but I am not one of your staff. This commission doesn't mean *that* much to me, I assure you. I have a meeting in a half hour, and I need to prepare. Your time is up."

He pressed a button on his screen, standing from the table, and for just a moment, I thought he was going to demand to speak to Mr. Cumberland.

"Are you allowed to speak to me like that?" he asked, one brow raised.

Truth was, I had no idea. Reality was, I didn't care. I needed this job, but there was no way Cumberland was going to fire me. I'd built well over half of the company's client list. I was insanely good at my job. But at the current moment, my health had to come first. I needed to pump, and it just couldn't wait.

"I guess we'll find out," I said, keeping my eyes locked on his. I wouldn't waver. I held out a hand, gesturing toward the door. I should've said it was nice to meet him, at the very least, but it wasn't, and I wasn't planning to lie.

He shoved his phone into his pocket before adjusting his blazer and walking around the table. When he stopped in front of me, he held out a hand. I stared at it.

"I'm very sorry to have wasted your time, Ms. Lewis. I'll have my secretary email you with the details of what I would like." His smoky eyes drilled into mine, a slight grin on his lips.

"Y-you're still hiring me?" I asked, accepting his hand. His grip was firm, and he nodded solemnly.

"I didn't get where I am by letting people walk all over me, either. I respect the fighter attitude, Ms. Lewis. Even when it's me you're fighting."

I nodded, unsure of what to say.

"If you ever decide to leave this place, let me know. We have openings for people with your attitude."

"Thank you. I'm going to be opening my own business soon," I said. I don't know why I told him. Perhaps to gain further praise. Perhaps to show I didn't need him.

"Well, if you need investors…" He pulled a card from his pocket.

"Th-thank you, Mr. Anderson." I suddenly felt incredibly embarrassed for my outburst.

"Don't back down, Ms. Lewis. It's that fighter spirit I'm betting on. Don't lose it." With that, he walked past me, phone already out, and he was gone.

From her office, Dannika stood, thumbs up, a question on her expression. I looked down, noticing the dark patches on my blazer. I didn't have time to talk. I hurried to my own office and grabbed my bags, then walked back to hers. I passed by Mr. Cumberland's office, staring through the glass walls. His office was double the size of the rest of the offices, but unlike ours, his was empty. Impersonal. Plain. He had no family or friends to boast about on his walls. He barely looked up from his phone call, waving at me as I walked past.

"I'm heading out," I told her. Her eyes traveled to the stains when I moved my arm from in front of my chest.

"Oh, my God. Do you need a jacket?"

"Do you have one?" I asked.

She jumped up, pulling hers from the back of her chair

and wrapping it around me. "There you go. What happened?"

"We got the deal, but it took longer than expected," I said. "I'll fill you in tomorrow, okay? I just need to get to the car."

"Pump while you drive, if you need to. I had to do it plenty of times."

"Will you let Cumberland know I'm leaving early?"

"Honey, you just secured the biggest client of the year. Cumberland should be kissing your feet." She giggled, tossing her braids over her shoulder. "Get home and snuggle that baby for me, okay?"

I nodded and darted from the office, planning to do just that.

Thirty-five minutes later, I parallel parked in front of the apartment building and pulled the bags of milk from my pump, careful not to spill any. I placed them carefully into the cooler, shoving my breasts back into my bra and stepping from the car. I crossed the quiet street and hurried up the stairs, twisting my key in the knob.

The apartment was eerily quiet.

"Ben?" I called in a whisper, setting my bags down on the sofa. I crossed through the living room and kitchen and down the hall, heading into the bedroom. "Are you guys napping?" I pushed open the bedroom door, my blood running cold. *"Ben?"*

The room was empty. I stepped back into the hall, pushing open the bathroom door. It was empty, too. Where were they?

The nursery was silent, no signs of life anywhere.

"Ben?" I called louder. Where could they be?

I walked back into the kitchen, opening the fridge. Gray's milk was still in the fridge, only two bags missing.

I pulled my phone from my pocket and clicked on his name in my recent calls. My hands were shaking as I lifted the phone to my ear, ice-cold fear shooting through my body. The nagging feeling that something definitely was not right was back, rearing its ugly head with the memory of the suspicious phone call.

"Hey, it's Ben. Sorry, I can't come to the phone right now…"

I hung up, a lump in my throat.

Where is my baby?

CHAPTER FIVE

I dialed his number again, this time walking back toward the door. I was prepared to head to the police station, dial 911, something. Anything. Everything felt like simultaneously an overreaction and an underreaction.

It rang once before I heard his voice. This time, it wasn't a recording.

"Hello?"

His voice sent shockwaves through me. *"Ben?"*

"Palmer? What's wrong?" he asked, his tone full of worry.

"Where are you?" I demanded, shaking.

"I took Gray to the park… Where are you?"

"To the park? He's not even two weeks old, Ben."

"Well, I didn't put him on the slide, Palm. I just wanted to get out of the house, get some fresh air. Are you okay?"

"No, I'm not okay. I'm home and freaking out because you were gone."

"You're home?" he asked, sounding out of breath.

"Yeah, I came home early, and you were gone."

"I'm sorry, babe," he said with a light chuckle. "We're almost home. I was planning to be home and have supper cooked before you got there."

I sank down on the couch. "I was so scared, Ben."

"What did you think happened? We ran away?"

"I didn't know what to think."

"The stroller was missing," he said, and I glanced to the place in the corner where the brand new green stroller had been sitting before. "You should've known I took him somewhere."

"I didn't know the two were related."

He snorted, trying to get me to laugh. "Wait, so you thought someone kidnapped the two of us *and* someone else broke in and stole the stroller, and the two were unrelated?"

"I hate you." I laughed. "God, I was so worried."

"I'm sorry we worried you, sweetheart. I'm walking up to the building now. See you in a minute."

I stood up, wiping my tears away and hanging my purse on the coat rack. I grabbed the cooler, placing the bags of milk into the freezer and unpacking the lunch I'd merely picked at. When I heard their footsteps outside the door, my heart swelled with joy, and when he stepped inside, I could've cried again. I pulled Gray into my arms, scaring him so badly he began to cry, though he immediately calmed when he realized it was me.

"He missed you, Mama," Ben said. He looked at my shirt, where white, dried milk stains now showed. "What happened?"

"I leaked because a client meeting ran too long."

"Cumberland knows you have to keep a schedule to keep your supply up," he said.

I rolled my eyes at his insistence that it should be that easy. "Cumberland couldn't care less about my supply, but this wasn't really his fault. As much as I hate to admit it."

"Even so, babe. You have rights. Whatever happens, you have to keep your supply up. It's what's best for Gray."

"I know that," I snapped, feeling like I was being scolded. I glanced down at the stroller as he wheeled it away from me without folding it up. "What's that?" In the basket underneath the stroller was a small, blue bag with green tissue paper sticking out the top.

He looked down, and I was nearly positive I'd seen a hint of dread on his face. "This?" He pulled the bag out and held it up. "Jason brought it by earlier. A gift for Gray."

"What is it?"

He pulled the tissue paper out and revealed a small onesie with a cute, smiling Earth on its belly. **Hi, I'm new here.**

I forced a stiff smile. "It's cute. This was really sweet of him."

"I thought so. Hopefully he can still fit in it, this chunkster." He laughed, rubbing Gray's belly.

"Why did you take it with you to the park?" I asked as Ben moved past me.

He spun back around. "What—oh, I didn't. I mean, I did, but…when I said he brought it here, I just meant I ran into him outside. He was bringing it by, but he hadn't told me. I just happened to catch him leaving the building, and I didn't want to have to come back upstairs."

I nodded, but I didn't believe it. I was fighting so hard against my instincts because of my past relationship. It had no place here. Nate was Nate and Ben was Ben, and they were not the same. "Well, please tell him thank you for me. Here, let me wash my hands. I want to feed him."

I hurried to the sink and scrubbed my hands before returning to Ben's side and taking my son. I sank into the couch, happily obliging his hungrily bobbing head.

Ben made himself a glass of water, wiping his forehead with the back of his hand once he'd finished gulping it down. "I was thinking pizza for dinner. What sounds good to you?"

"Pizza's fine," I said, rubbing a finger across Gray's cheeks. It was the first time I'd felt at peace all day.

"Excellent. I'm going to take a shower before I get it started." With that, he disappeared down the hall, leaving Gray and me alone. It wasn't until I heard the water running that I realized he hadn't kissed me hello. That was a first.

BEN AND GRAY were sound asleep on the couch while I typed away on my computer. Anderson's secretary had sent over a list of his requests, and I was busy drafting my proposal for his event. It would easily be a quarter of a million. I shuddered as the bill continued to rise with each new estimate. It was more than my salary, on an event that would last half a day. Sometimes my job made me sick.

I looked over at my husband, peacefully sleeping with

Gray on his chest. I couldn't pretend it didn't bother me that they'd left the house without telling me, but it was irrational to be mad. Ben was in charge of his care. Of course they'd be going places without letting me know. So why was it bothering me so much?

I closed the laptop and laid it on the coffee table, standing up. Ben had finished up the dishes, but the dish towel lay on the counter. I grabbed it and walked to the bathroom. His clothes lay on the floor. I knew he'd get them in the morning, this wasn't my job anymore, but it still bothered me. I couldn't sink into a nice, luxurious bath while a pile of dirty clothes sat festering on the floor. I scooped them up, walking toward the bedroom to put them into the hamper, but groaned when I realized it was already overflowing. He needed to start a load, but he was exhausted. I pushed the anger from my mind, smiling sadly at the spit-up covered shirt on top of the pile.

Sighing, I heaved the hamper into the hallway and opened the washer. I tossed the dish towel in first, then reached in his pants pocket and pulled out change, a tissue, and a receipt before throwing his pants and shirt in as well. I laid the pile on top of the dryer and began sorting through the hamper, separating our clothes from Gray's. When the laundry had been started, I grabbed the receipt, ready to throw it away and toss the change in Gray's piggy bank when I looked it over.

Gary's Grill

It was date stamped for that day at noon. He'd stopped for lunch.

I'd never heard of the place, but the address showed it

was a few blocks from the park. My eyes trailed down the receipt, a sinking feeling in my stomach.

Why had he ordered two meals?

I forced myself to inhale a sharp breath. I couldn't panic. I walked back to our bedroom and put the hamper away with shaking hands, then shoved the receipt into my pajama pants pocket before returning to the living room. I touched his arm, causing him to stir.

He sniffed, rubbing his eyes before he opened them. He looked at me, then around the room, then down at his chest where Gray lay.

"Are you ready for bed?" I asked.

"Mhm," he said as I lifted Gray. "Sorry, I didn't mean to fall asleep."

"You had a long day."

"Not as long as yours," he said, shifting his weight around so he could sit up. "Did you finish the show?"

I shook my head. "I turned it off when you started snoring. I had emails to deal with anyway, and I didn't want you to miss it."

He kissed my cheek. "Thanks, babe." When he stood, he stretched, then lifted his coffee cup from the end table and walked it to the sink. Noticing I hadn't moved, he walked back toward me. "Is everything okay?"

"What all did you do today?" I asked, trying to keep my voice lighter than the weight I felt in my chest.

"What do you mean?" He sat down on the coffee table across from me, seeming concerned, albeit sleepy.

"When you were out."

"We...went to the park. Walked around for a bit... walked around the neighborhood."

"That was it?"

His eyes narrowed at me, his expression conflicted between laughter and confusion. "I think so... Why do you ask?"

I folded my hands across my chest. "Did you go out to eat?"

He was still for a moment, then recognition filled his expression. "I grabbed lunch at a little restaurant near the park, yeah. How did you know?"

"Just you?"

"Well, I took Gray, obviously. As much as he wanted to stay behind...Palmer, you're scaring me. What's this about?" He reached for my knee, his finger tracing the pattern on my pants.

I pulled the receipt from my pocket. "Were you hungry enough to eat two meals?"

His brows knit together as he reached for the receipt, reading it over. When he looked up at me, his eyes were wide. "I forgot, I'm sorry. I...paid it forward, or whatever it's called. There was a woman there with a young girl, maybe four or five. She ordered the girl's meal but didn't have enough for her own. I felt bad. It was just a couple bucks, Palm. I didn't think you'd mind."

My hands were shaking, my stomach tight as I stared at him, trying to decide whether to trust him. He'd never given me any reason not to. Besides the suspicious phone call, I guessed.

"She told you she couldn't afford it?"

"No. Of course not. She wasn't like...a panhandler or anything. She didn't even want to take it when I offered." He shook his head, standing from the table. "She ordered two meals, but when they told her the total, she asked them to take hers off. I just figured...I'd hope someone would help you out if it were you there without enough money." It was reasonable enough, I couldn't deny it. "Becoming a dad has softened me, I guess," he teased. "You aren't mad, are you? I know it's your money."

"It's not *my* money, Ben. We talked about this. It's both of ours. And, of course, I'm not mad. I just...I was worried you were cheating on me or something."

His expression went cold with shock, and he shook his head once again, leaning in so his forehead rested on mine. "Hey," he said. "I could never cheat on you. I'm not that guy, Palmer. You know that. I know you were hurt in the past...but I would never do that to you. I love you so much."

"I love you, too," I whispered, feeling tears well in my eyes. I hated talking about my past, but we both knew it affected everything I did then. Being cheated on after an eight-year relationship causes everything you thought you knew to go to shreds. I'd only recently begun to accept myself again. Ben coming along a year ago, Ben loving me like he had... It saved me. He saved me. Gray was our surprise, but Ben hadn't run away. He'd loved me through all of it. Married me. Fallen for me despite my growing belly and flaws. I felt more foolish than ever. Of course he wasn't cheating. "I'm sorry."

"You don't have to be sorry, sweetheart. Just trust me, okay? I have no reason to cheat. You're perfect." He kissed my forehead, then lifted my chin to meet my lips. I kissed him back, the ice in my intestines warming quickly. We still weren't cleared to have sex yet, which only made this torture. He lifted his hands up to my neck, drawing out our kiss. When we broke apart, he rested his forehead on mine for another second. "I love you."

"I love *you*," I told him.

"Now, what do you say the three of us get to bed?" he asked, breaking away with a yawn and a laugh. I stood in agreement, yawning as well and following him toward the bedroom.

I loved Ben. I trusted Ben. But I couldn't deny the nagging feeling that reminded me I'd trusted and been burned before.

CHAPTER SIX

The next morning, I walked out the front door with a few less tears than the day before. I'd chosen a dark, patterned shirt to prevent any leaks showing. I was more prepared, ready to deal with whatever came my way. Or, so I thought.

I crossed the street and climbed into my car, glancing up at the window of our apartment. The curtain moved, like maybe they were going to wave goodbye, but no one was there. The pit in my stomach was back. Had he been watching to see me leave?

I didn't want to be weighed down by all that had happened to me. I didn't want to be fearful in every relationship I was in, but I had to deal with the feelings I was having. I had to prove to myself Ben wasn't cheating—wasn't *going* to cheat. I had to trust him, but I had to make myself believe I could.

Still, I pulled away from the apartment building, but rather than turning left to head to work, I went up a street further and made a U-turn. I pulled into the parking lot of another apartment building, parking in a visitor's parking space. I texted Cumberland, letting him know I might be a little late. I had no idea how long I needed to sit and wait, how long I'd even be allowed to sit and wait. Until the lump in my throat disappeared, I supposed.

Luckily—or rather unluckily, however you chose to look at it—for me, I didn't have to wait long. After twenty minutes had passed, the front door of my apartment building opened, and I watched as the familiar lime green and gray stroller came into view. Ben was on his phone, talking away as he turned the corner, oblivious to me watching him.

I pulled out when he'd disappeared from view, driving slowly and keeping my distance, turning down streets full minutes after him. He walked past the park, not stopping, and continued on toward the next set of apartments. Was he going to visit someone? If so, who? His family lived out of state and, as far as I knew, he didn't have any friends in Oceanside. Apparently, I'd been wrong.

He kept walking past the apartment, and finally I realized where he was headed. The red and white sign came into view. **Gary's Grill.**

It was a rundown, outdated building with dull, white parking lot lines that needed to be repainted, and smoke billowing from the vent on the roof. It was not any place I would've chosen. There was an awning, where the kitchen could be seen; you could choose to order and either eat inside or out. Ben walked to a picnic table with Gray, taking a seat outside.

I parallel parked behind a white work van, my view only partially obstructed. *What are they doing?*

I wrung my hands in my lap, watching with an uneasy feeling as Ben continued talking on the phone, occasionally putting his hands in the stroller to soothe Gray.

After a few moments, Ben stood, his eyes locked with something in the distance. The smile on his face was wide, warm, and utterly heartbreaking.

I followed his gaze to where a woman approached from the opposite side of town. She had strawberry-blonde hair, her roots dark brown, and wore blue jean shorts and a tiny, white cami with no bra. She was smiling as she grew nearer, her arms outstretched as my husband pulled her into an embrace.

I watched in pure horror as the scene unfolded. *Not again. Please, not again.*

I was going to be sick, I was sure of it. My body was tense, tears blurring my vision as I watched her take a seat next to Ben on the picnic bench, both of them cooing over my baby in the stroller. He kept one arm around her, smiling proudly as she reached in, touching Gray.

My hands balled into fists, my whole body shaking with adrenaline and anger. Everything in me wanted to shove open the door, run over there, grab the stroller, and run, but I had to remain calm. I had to do better, be better than last time.

When I'd caught Nate cheating, I'd made a complete and utter fool of myself. Making a huge scene at that bar hadn't gotten me anywhere. I had to control myself this time. Learn from my mistakes.

I pulled out my phone, clicking on his name in my messages and typing something slowly. My shaking hands made for many errors, but eventually, I had the message ready. *Send.*

How is he?

I watched Ben carefully, spying down to the second when the message came through. He lifted his phone from the picnic table, staring at it with incredulity. A waiter approached their table, and I watched them order. When the waiter left, the woman said something, and he laughed before responding.

Just finished eating and now he's laying down.

So, he *was* lying. Already. Even if there was some way to explain his way through this. He was lying to me. About who knew how much. Who was this woman? Why was he meeting her?

Send me a picture? I miss you both already.

He read the message as it came through, but laid his phone down, obviously conflicted. When the waiter approached again, this time with two baskets of food, Ben paid in cash. I swallowed. We never used cash. In fact, it was rare that we even had it.

I pulled my wallet from my purse, chill bumps lining my skin as I opened it and gasped. The forty dollars I kept in my purse for emergencies was gone.

He'd stolen from me.

As much as I swore the money was ours, that he could spend whatever he needed to, it still stung. We were lucky enough to be well taken care of thanks to my job, but I didn't want him literally taking money from my wallet. Maybe it was selfish of me to feel that way.

Buzz.

I looked down at the newest text message. **I'm getting**

ready to jump in the shower. I'll text you one soon. Miss you too.

I glanced out the window, barely able to see them through my blurry, tear-filled vision. Gray was out of his stroller now, balanced in the woman's arms as she shoved a fry into her mouth, bouncing my child on her knee. Ben kissed the top of his head, looking carefree.

A scream bubbled in my chest, ready to rip free. I wanted to attack. I swallowed it down, just barely.

Instead, I watched.

CHAPTER SEVEN

Ben stayed with the woman for around an hour, the three of them looking like a perfect little family. When they parted, he pressed his lips to her head, though only briefly. She kissed Gray's head, whispering in his ear before she walked away, climbing into a beat-up, red Honda.

When she pulled away, Ben loaded Gray into the stroller and, together, they headed back toward the apartment. I considered following them, letting him know he'd been caught, but I wondered if he'd attempt to lie again. I needed to know everything I could about this woman before I told Ben I knew anything.

So, I followed the woman instead. We drove away from downtown, then away from the outskirts of town and out of Oceanside altogether. The midday traffic wasn't nearly rush hour, so I found it easy to keep track of her. I had a text from Dannika waiting on my phone, asking if everything was all right, but I couldn't respond. I had to keep my focus.

She exited the interstate toward Crestview with just three cars in between us. I'd never been to the tiny town of Crestview, though it was just under an hour from my apartment. We drove past a small diner, past a rundown barber shop, a few abandoned buildings, and a vet clinic, past the small park, and down a long, twisted street with no sidewalk. The Spanish moss hung in the trees, making the neighborhood picturesque. It was everything I loved about North Carolina and the South in general. If I weren't so focused, so angry, so hurt, I may have been able to appreciate it more.

Finally, she pulled into a small, one-story house with white, metal siding and black shutters. I drove past, turning on the next street and making a lap around the block. There was nowhere on the quiet street for me to park that wouldn't draw attention to myself. I drove slowly back toward the house just in time to see her front door shut. Knowing where she lived wasn't enough. I needed to know her. I needed to know why she was better than me.

I pulled the car over to park three houses down from hers on the side of the road and walked back toward her house. From the angle I was standing, I could see a tree house in her backyard. I looked around the neighborhood. There was no one outside, no blinds pulled sideways as they tried to decide what this stranger was doing there. I hurried up the sidewalk and down the privacy fence of her neighbor, toward her backyard. It was a miracle I made it without being stopped, but I did.

It was the middle of the day, and I was finely dressed. If I were to get stopped, I was hopeful I'd be able to lie my way out of any trouble. I walked along the back of her house, careful with each step, looking for dogs or any signs of kids or a husband. There were none. The back patio was scattered with leaves, and I was careful to make quiet steps as I walked across. The blinds were all drawn up, giving me a clear view into the house, but, at the same time, it gave her a clear view out. I needed to determine where she was, so I could decide whether climbing into the tree house would be safe. I didn't want to be caught.

The ladder to the tree house was on the back side of the tree, facing away from the house, and without allowing myself to second-guess my decision, I launched forward, digging my heels into the soggy ground and throwing myself against the tree. I looked out to the side, staring into the windows of the house. It was small and quaint. Sparsely decorated. There was a single couch in the open-concept living room and a small, plain kitchen. She was standing at the counter, talking on the phone with her back to me.

I climbed the ladder, my heels slipping on each mildewy piece of board, and I pulled myself up into the tiny tree house In the corner, a wasp buzzed. Normally, I would've run away from it, but at that moment, I was too laser-focused on my anger.

I walked toward the edge of the tree house nearest the house, my pants covered in dirt. There was no way I could go into the office now, regardless, so I was no longer concerned with the time. The walls and branches gave me a perfect hideaway up here. I was protected, but she was not. I could see directly into the house, though she could no longer see me.

With sudden relief, I sank down to the floor, watching carefully as she ended the phone call, laying her phone down on the counter and walking toward the cabinet. She opened it and grabbed a jar of peanut butter, pulling a spoon from the drawer and beginning to eat straight from the jar, seemingly lost in thought.

She wasn't beautiful, and I didn't think it was judgy to say so. She was plain, with frizzy hair and eyes that were too close together. She had a better figure than I did, her waist much smaller, hips slightly wider, but smaller breasts. Much smaller than mine now that I was nursing.

She had freckles across her shoulders while mine were creamy smooth. I wanted to pick her apart, find any and all flaws with her, because I had to know why he'd chosen her, and I had to believe he'd chosen wrong.

Buzz. Buzz.

A scream nearly escaped my throat as my phone buzzed in my pocket, breaking up the tension. I stood, trying to calm my shaking hands as I pulled it out.

The office.

"H-hello?" I said, keeping my voice low.

"Hey, babe, where are you?" It was Dannika.

"I had to go to a client meeting this morning," I lied. "Is everything okay?"

"Everything's more than okay," she said in a singsong voice. "Your little cutie came by to see you."

My heart plummeted, and I grasped onto the wall of the tree house, pulling myself up. "What?"

"Ben's here. He brought Gray by for a visit. Should I tell him it'll be awhile? Are you close?"

I trembled with fear, the lump in my stomach metastasizing as cold fear traveled through my body at breakneck speed. I wasn't sure I'd ever feel calm again. Not with all I knew—all I was hiding. All *he* was hiding. "Tell him I'll be there soon. I'm just wrapping up."

"Sure thing." She clicked her tongue. "I'll see you soon."

I nodded, though she couldn't see me, and let the phone slide down away from my ear.

Ben hadn't texted or called. Why on earth was he at my office? My phone screen reverted to my normal background—a photo of the three of us, letting me know the call had disconnected, but I could only hear her words ringing in my ears.

Ben's here.

CHAPTER EIGHT

I rushed into the office, hair flying, pants covered in dirt. I dusted my legs off with each step, practically falling over myself as I went.

"Slow down. Where's the fire?" Howie asked, lowering the headset from his ear. "Oh, wait, he's in your office." He winked, pointing me toward my office, where I could see the outline of my husband sitting across from my desk through the frosted glass.

"Did he say what he's doing here?" I asked, keeping my voice low.

Howie shook his head slowly. "I...no. Should I have asked? Dannika was the one who talked to him. I didn't know."

"No, it's fine," I assured him, trying to seem less concerned than I was. I could count on one hand the number of times Ben had showed up at my office, and never without warning.

"The baby's cuter than you, by the way," Howie teased as I walked past, and I cast a grin back at him that I hoped looked playful.

I pushed my office door open, dread sitting heavy in my stomach. What was he doing here? What did he know? Why should I feel guilty when I'd done nothing wrong? *Nothing short of trespassing, anyway.*

Ben stood, looking me over as he leaned in to give me a hug. I held my breath in fear I'd catch a whiff of an unfamiliar perfume and it would break me. I couldn't break down right now. I had to stay strong. "Hey, honey. Sorry to surprise you like this."

"Hey." My voice was so sugary sweet it nearly made me sick. "No, don't be silly. I'm glad to see you. I'm just sorry you had to wait. Is everything okay?" I hugged him back, then lowered myself to Gray's stroller, where he was sleeping peacefully. *Big day for the both of them.*

"Yeah, yeah," Ben said, shoving his hands in his pockets with a deep, drawn-out inhale. "Everything's fine. He was extra fussy this morning, so I thought I'd take him for a drive. You didn't mention you'd be out of the office."

I stood, one brow raised. Was he really questioning where *I'd* been? "I don't normally tell you my schedule." I laughed at the end, attempting to make my statement less abrasive. "What else have you done today?" I waited, barely breathing. It felt like a game, both of us teasing and toying with each other to see what would be revealed. I wasn't sure if I was the only one playing.

His eyes darted toward the floor, and I could swear he grew a shade paler. "Nothing, really. I fed him some breakfast, and then we headed here."

I glanced at the Apple Watch on my wrist. "It's been

two hours since I left. Surely you've done something besides feeding him breakfast."

"What would we have done?" he asked, meeting my eyes finally. After a moment, he cleared his throat. "We were slow moving, I'll admit. Traffic was pretty bad, but we hung around the house for a while after breakfast while I tried to keep him calm."

"What's wrong with him?" I asked, my concentration momentarily pulled to my child from my cheating husband. "Why was he fussing?" Gray was usually a happy baby—*oh wait*. I reminded myself he was lying. Gray hadn't been fussy at all when they were at the park. This was all an excuse. Why was my gut instinct to trust him even when I knew it was a lie?

"I think he just had a bit of gas. The car ride seemed to help," Ben said, grabbing a piece of cinnamon candy from the small bowl on my desk. He unwrapped it and popped it into his mouth. "Did we interrupt you with a client?"

"I'd just finished up."

"It looks like you got something on your pants." He pointed to the stains on my suit.

"I know." I walked around toward my seat and opened a drawer, pulling out a Tide pen and rubbing it over the stains I could see. I was trying to hide my anger, trying to distract myself, when all I really wanted to do was confront him, lash out, and make a scene. I wanted to tell him all I knew, all I'd seen, and all I wanted to do to him. But my child was sleeping just feet away. I was in my place of business. For the sake of women everywhere, I had to do better. I had to represent us better. "The meeting was outside, and the client had kids." I didn't explain further, and he didn't pry. An outdoor meeting, plus children, equals stains—self-explanatory.

"So, do you want to grab lunch with us?" he asked, twisting his mouth as he sucked on the candy.

I did want to go. I wanted to be with Gray, to talk to Ben, more than I wanted anything else. Two things were keeping me at work, though. One being that I honestly did need to catch up on things. Over half of my unread emails from yesterday were still sitting in my inbox. I also didn't think I could control myself around him yet. I needed time to process what I'd discovered today. Time to regain my composure. When I confronted him, I wanted to be calm, to stay calm, so I wouldn't let him manipulate me. The more stressed I got with Nate, the more he could lead the conversation and make me believe what he was saying. It wasn't until we were apart that I would realize he'd steered the conversation his way, negating the issues I was bringing up. I wouldn't make those same mistakes with Ben. I sighed, patting my hands on the desk. "I really shouldn't. I need to catch up on a few things. Maybe tomorrow?"

His expression was distant, not quite sad, but there was an emotion there I didn't recognize. "Yeah, okay." He sat down across from me, waiting. "Dannika just loves Gray."

"Why wouldn't she?" I cooed, staring at the stroller. "He's perfect."

Ben chuckled, rubbing a hand through his hair. "That's true. We did make a pretty amazing kid." He paused, seeming conflicted. "Hey, Palm?"

I flicked my eyes back toward him. "Yeah?"

"We're...we're okay, right?"

I stared at him, blinking once, twice, before I answered. He was on edge. Nervous. But I couldn't figure out why. Was it just a guilty conscience? Had he seen my car following him? Had I been caught catching him? If so, he'd have to admit it. I wouldn't fold. Not yet.

"Why would you ask that?" I picked up a pen from the side of my desk, clicking it slowly to keep my hands busy.

"I...I just wanted to be sure. You seemed strange this morning," he told me. His words were slow, as if he were testing the waters of how I'd react. I gave him nothing.

I blinked, my lips forming a tight, unaffected smile. "What do you mean? I don't think I acted strangely this morning."

"I don't know. I can't explain it. I just...I get the feeling you're...avoiding me, or something. Did I do anything wrong?" All signs pointed to a guilty conscience.

"I'm not avoiding you, Ben," I said, my voice light and airy. "Why would you think that? *Should* I be avoiding you? You're the one acting strangely now."

He swallowed with a light, forced laugh. "No, of course not. I'm sorry. I'm being ridiculous. I just wanted to be sure. I guess I just...feel weird. I know we said we were both okay with me staying home with Gray, but I know your first day back was horrible. I'm worried about you. Worried about what you think of me. You know I can go back if that's what you'd rather have me do. If you want to be home with him."

I took a deep breath, clasping my hands together in front of me. "I appreciate you checking on me, but I'm honestly okay. I mean, yes, it's hard being away from him.

Yes, I'd rather be home, but we both said this was what's best. I make more than you. I can provide us with insurance. Besides, I love what I do. I've worked hard to get where I am, and Dannika and I still plan to open our own firm one day. To quit now would mean giving all of that up. It's not easy, I won't lie, but I love that you get to be home with him." *Loved.* "It feels safer than daycare, and I want you two to bond." *With each other, not random park sluts.*

It was the strangest conversation, my inner thoughts fighting with everything I was telling him. As angry as I was, I felt like I needed to keep it together. I needed to know more about Ben's indiscretions, in case I was wrong about what I'd seen, though I highly doubted that was the case. I didn't want to be acting based on my experiences with my cheating ex. Ben wasn't Nate. If he was cheating, I needed to know the truth and, until I did, I couldn't react. I had to keep myself in line, even if he wasn't. It was a fine line to walk. Dannika had told me too many horror stories about her husband, Ty's, divorce cases. The amount of alimony paid to spouses, the way the assets were split. I didn't want to go through a divorce, didn't want to lose my husband or my money, if there was a way to ease my fears and prove myself wrong.

He let out a sigh, his shoulders sinking with relief. "Okay, good. I just wanted to be sure."

He seemed lighter now, his face a pale pink and illuminated. It was as if he may float up to my ceiling if I didn't hold him down. "Was that why you came by?"

He nodded hesitantly. "Sort of, yeah."

"Ben, you could've called and asked," I said as he stood, our visit obviously at an end.

"I know, but I really did want to see you." *Is he lying? Is he always?*

I stood too, leaning into his kiss as he leaned over the desk toward me. At the last moment, I turned my head slightly, so his lips landed on the corner of my mouth. I looked at Gray. "I love you."

Ben backed up, gripping the stroller's handles. "We love you, too, Mama." I stepped toward the door and pulled it open so they could pass through, running my hand over my sleeping child cautiously. They made their way toward the door, being greeted by enthusiastic waves and silent goodbyes from my coworkers, each enchanted by the beautiful baby I'd made with the best liar I knew.

If he thought he could continue to lie to me, he was in for a surprise. I'd find out the truth, and I'd use it to ruin him. I wasn't going to be betrayed again. I'd let myself get walked all over for months before gaining the courage to walk away. I'd worked too hard to build myself up again to let another man destroy me. I'd learned my lesson with Nate. It was time for Ben to learn his.

CHAPTER NINE

When I made it home that afternoon, the apartment smelled of warming cheese and spices, a sure sign that Ben had a casserole in the oven.

I pushed open the front door, shocked to see them lying on the floor. Ben held Gray over his head, laughing as the baby giggled in his arms. "Hey, sweet boy," I said, dropping to the floor next to them. Ben pursed his lips, waiting for a kiss, but I pretended not to see, turning my attention to Gray immediately. "Did you have a good day?" I took him from Ben's arms, and he sat up, not missing a beat and resting his back against the couch. "Was he fussy any more?"

Ben shook his head. "Say 'not at all, Mama,'" he teased. "He was the perfect angel."

"Of course he was." I rocked back and forth, patting his back as he bobbed against my shoulder. "He's a little gentleman, aren't you?" I said, moving to stand up and lifting my nose in the air. "What's for dinner?"

"Broccoli and chicken casserole," Ben said, pushing up

from the couch and making his way into the kitchen. I could hear the oven open without turning around to see him do it. "And it looks about done. How was your day?"

I nodded, kissing Gray's head. "Smells delicious." When I turned around, Ben was placing a potholder on the counter. "My day was fine, nothing too exciting. They all raved over Gray after you left."

Ben gave a crooked smile as he pulled the casserole from the oven and fanned a hand over it. I could see the cheese bubbling from where I stood.

"He was fine the rest of the afternoon. No more fussing, no more gas. I guess he just needed to see you." He spun around, opening the fridge and pulling out a pitcher of fresh lemonade. It was my dinner drink of choice throughout my pregnancy and now that I was nursing, and Ben made sure to always have a fresh glass ready for me. He set it down. I was so conflicted, finding it hard to find the line between this man who doted on me, waited on me hand and foot while I was recovering, cried when he held our son for the first time, and the man who would throw that all away to cheat on me. Throughout our time together, Ben had been the perfect way for me to get over my disastrous end with Nate. He'd been everything Nate wasn't. Kind, compassionate, understanding, a great listener, and, most importantly, I thought he'd been honest. We had the hard conversations up front. He knew about my past, and though he didn't like to talk much about his own, I knew what mattered. I thought so, anyway. I thought I knew him. "You okay?" he asked, pulling me from my thoughts.

I nodded. "Sorry. I'm fine."

He stared at me for a moment, as if waiting for me to say more, then stepped back. "Okay. That needs to sit for about fifteen minutes, so I'm going to grab a shower if you're fine with that."

I couldn't tell him how okay with it I was, how much I needed him to give me space, so instead, I turned away with a small nod. He hurried down the hall and shut the bedroom, then bathroom door, and within moments I heard the shower kick on. I set my purse on the shelf near the door and carried Gray toward the couch, so thankful to have him in my arms again.

"I'm not mad at you," I teased him. "I know you couldn't help it." I smiled as he did. "No, I know. I know you didn't want to go see that horrible woman, did you? No, sweet boy."

I lowered him to my lap, propping my feet on the coffee table and playing with his soft little feet. His eyes traveled the room, taking it all in with wonder. At his age, he was seeing nothing more than spots of light, but it was exciting to see the way his eyes gravitated toward them. The window, the lights above the kitchen island. I followed his gaze, feeling curious about what the world looked like from his bright, blue eyes. So much less dark than from my own, I was sure. He didn't know the evils that existed. I prayed he'd never have to.

When my gaze landed on the coffee table, and on Ben's phone to be exact, I froze.

He'd forgotten his phone on the coffee table.

I glanced down the hall. The shower was still running.

Could I chance going through it?

Should I?

How long did I have? Ten minutes, at least.

I reached for the black iPhone, pulling it toward me and tapping in his password. *At least that hasn't changed.* I pulled up his messages first.

Palmer

Jason—his old boss

Dean—his coworker.

I clicked on the messages from Jason, looking for any form of congratulations or thank yous, but there were none. The last text was from a few months ago, when Ben had texted to say he was stuck in traffic and would be a few minutes late. It struck me as odd, though Ben had never said Jason texted him, only called, so I couldn't be too suspicious.

I scrolled through a few others, one from a beer delivery service, one from a man we'd bought a lamp from, some from a few more coworkers wishing us congratulations after Gray's birth. Nothing from any numbers or names I didn't recognize. I opened the text messages from the names I recognized, checking to be sure it really was them. I knew all the tricks. My ex had made sure of that.

Nothing out of the ordinary.

I opened his calls, scrolling back to just over a week ago when I'd overheard the conversation that Ben claimed was with Jason. Friday the fifth. I scrolled up and down, shaking my head. There were no calls on that day at all, which meant either the phone call hadn't happened, or it had and he'd deleted the true identity of the caller from his phone. The truth was obvious.

Next, I checked his Facebook and all the messages in

his Messenger. *Nothing.* It was likely he'd deleted his contact with her. Either that, or I really had overreacted. Perhaps she was just a familiar face from his past that he ran into. Nothing more than that. Perhaps he'd accidentally deleted the call from Jason, though that really made no sense.

Down the hall, he began singing. He was conditioning. It was a telltale sign.

As a last resort, I opened the Instagram app and searched through his messages there. A few random things that looked like spam, a few brand rep companies, and one message from an account that no longer existed.

He rarely used Instagram, so I wasn't all that surprised. I clicked on his profile, searching through his pictures for anyone who'd liked his pictures who resembled the girl, to no avail. He wasn't all that popular there, one or two likes on his total of sixteen posts, and she wasn't one of them. No one resembling the woman had ever liked or commented on any form of his social media. She was a ghost. I had no name, a vague recollection of her appearance, a knowledge of where she lived, though I hadn't made a point to remember her address, and that was it.

I clicked on the search button, ready to look for the restaurant, in case she worked there. Instead, my eyes widened.

What?

The water shut off down the hall, but I wasn't listening.

There, right at my fingertips, was her name. The last person he'd searched. KatieKat. Sunflower emoji next to her name. I clicked on her profile. The girl in the photograph looked much better than the one I'd seen today. She seemed younger and happier, with dark sunglasses, a polka dot headband, and a large, bubblegum bubble protruding from her lips.

I scrolled.

She ran a food and travel blog called KatieKatTravels, I was learning, where she traveled and blogged about the foods she tried. She was…incredibly popular, as it turned out. Each of her posts had well over a thousand comments and even more likes.

She was fun, playful, and annoyingly adorable.

Her latest post was an announcement that she was planning to try out a restaurant outside of Crestview for their grand opening. *Dilly Darlings.*

The bathroom door opened, causing me to jump. I cleared out of his phone right away, closing the app and tossing the phone down on the table just as he headed my way. I hadn't been quick enough, though.

"What were you doing?" he asked with a half-laugh. I wasn't sure what he'd seen.

"Looking through your phone."

He swallowed. "Okay…why?" To my surprise, he didn't seem angry.

I shrugged one shoulder nonchalantly. "Mine was in my purse, and I didn't want to get back up. I just scrolled through Facebook."

He nodded, not looking the least bit concerned, but he should've been. I knew his secrets, and I was prepared to expose them.

"Want me to grab it for you?" he asked, pointing toward my purse.

"Please." I tried to calm the adrenaline racing through me as he turned away. He walked over, the towel around his waist, and while I normally would've taken in the sight of my husband in a state of undress, I couldn't bring myself to do it. I didn't care. It all just hurt too badly. How could I appreciate his boyish charm and devilish good looks when I couldn't get the image of him holding her, him kissing her, out of my head?

He pulled my phone from my purse and tossed it toward me. "He fell asleep?" he asked, his hands resting on his hips.

"No, he's awake. He's just...being calm," I told him, looking down to Gray, who was staring into space, his little lips opening and closing. Everything was so simple for him. I was almost envious.

"You ready to eat?" he asked, heading back down the hall and toward our bedroom.

I was. I wanted to stay and eat, but I already knew I wasn't going to. I had somewhere else to be now. My stomach was growling and I desperately didn't want to leave Gray, but I had to know the truth. I had to. I'd been here before and brushed my suspicions away, and it had been to my own detriment. I wouldn't do it again.

"Actually," I said, an apology in my tone, "I'm not going to be able to have dinner with you. Howie just emailed me about a client. I'm going to have to go into the office for an hour."

He reappeared in the hall, this time dressed, and ran his towel over his wet hair. "What? Seriously? You just got home."

"I know," I told him, wincing. "Trust me, I wouldn't go

if I didn't have to. I'm starving and dinner smells delicious. But it's a really big client. I can't afford to let this event fall apart."

He sighed, tossing the towel into the laundry room and heading toward me with his arms outstretched. "Do you want me to make you some dinner to go? You must be starving."

"No, that's all right. I won't be able to eat it on the go, and I couldn't eat during the meeting, anyway. I'll be okay. Just…could you leave a plate out for me for when I get home?"

He took Gray from my arms, the all-too-familiar lump of worry reappearing in my belly. "Of course." He leaned in, kissing my lips before I could deflect, and I kissed Gray's head as well.

"Okay, I'll be back soon. I shouldn't be gone long." I turned away from him and scooped up my purse, heading out the door before I could talk myself out of my plan.

I CREATED A FAKE INSTAGRAM PROFILE, *Sarah Silver,* while sitting in the street in front of the restaurant and followed Katie, turning on the alerts so I'd get notified whenever she posted.

After I was done, I climbed from the car and walked into the restaurant, pulling out my phone once I'd been seated. I pretended to stare at the screen, while in reality, my eyes searched the room, trying to determine where she might be. According to her post, she should've been here. Had I missed her? Had she already come and gone? It had only been an hour since she'd made the post.

I checked back on her Instagram. There were no food pictures yet, nothing to announce that she'd actually been here.

Refresh.

Her feed now contained a new picture, a small, white plate on a red table, much like my own. *She is here.*

I turned in my seat, looking all around. Where was she? Why was I missing her? I stood, walking toward the bathroom. "Is everything all right, miss?" my waiter asked, stopping me.

"Yes, sorry. Everything's fine. I'm just going to eat at the bar, if that's all right? My date bailed."

He nodded, his wary smile warming. "Sure, of course."

I walked past him, past the booths of an older couple, and a much younger couple, then the table of a group of teens who looked entirely annoyed about everything in their lives.

When I rounded the corner, I stopped in my tracks. There she was. *Katie.* My husband's mistress.

I stood completely frozen for a moment as I processed what was happening. She was dressed much better, her hair frizz-free and curled into beachy, shoulder-length waves. She wore high-waist shorts and a pink tube top that matched the pink ribbons attached to her shoes and running up her calves. She took a bite of the cheesecake in front of her, chewing with intention, her eyes closed.

When they opened, I moved to the side, hiding slightly behind the partition of glass and alcohol just in time for her to look my way. If she saw me, she didn't react.

Instead, she took another bite. She turned her phone around, holding the fork up parallel to her face and grinning wildly.

Within minutes, the picture was online, and I was staring at the photo—her teeth a bit whiter, her face a bit filtered. The cheesecake has been rated six out of five *cherries*, whatever that meant.

I groaned, trying to lean further and further around the partition so I could get a better look at her. Here, she was pretty. Here, she was more of a threat, and I could finally see what he saw in her. The realization was a gut punch, a tearing open of the wounds I fought so hard to staple closed after Nate left.

Within moments, she stood, dropping 2 one-dollar bills beside the plate, taking a sip of the pink drink in front of her and walking from the restaurant, her nose buried in her phone.

Just like she'd appeared in my life, in a flash, she was gone.

CHAPTER TEN

I'd left my apartment early the next morning, already positioned in front of the woman's house when she walked from its doors. I was becoming obsessed with her, but I couldn't stop. After Ben had gone to bed, I'd spent most of the night staring at her pictures, reading her captions, trying to picture her voice.

Over and over the question rang out in my head: *why are you better than me?*

This time, she was dressed like she was when I'd first seen her, in a tiny tank top and shorts. This time, though, instead of heading toward Oceanside, she drove toward downtown Crestview. The small, rundown town square boasted very few businesses, but she pulled up in front of a small beauty shop, and climbed from her car.

I slowed to a stop in the parking lot across from her, watching to see what was going to happen. The windows were tinted, but I could see her frame as she flitted across the room, taking a seat beside a woman already waiting.

She didn't speak to anyone, from what I could see, so I assumed they must know her there.

The shop, *Sassy Snips*, was small and white, with large, pink letters painted on the front windows. There was a painted picture of a pair of scissors beside the name. I dialed the number printed on the door and waited.

"Sassy Snips, this is Carolyn." A loud, friendly voice answered the phone with laughter in her tone. Almost as if I'd caught her midway through a joke.

I cleared my throat. "Hi, um, I was wondering if you require appointments or if you take walk-ins."

"Oh, no, hun. We take walk-ins."

"Oh, excellent. Thank you." I pressed the button, ending the call without saying goodbye, and stepped out of the car. When I walked into the building, I smelled bleach, masked by a floral shampoo. It was quaint and simple, concrete floors and large, bright can lights in the ceiling. There were three seats along each exterior wall and six shampoo stations in the center, back to back.

"Hi, hun, can I help you?" A blonde woman looked up from an elderly man's haircut, scissors held at the ready.

"I…I don't have an appointment. I just wanted to get a trim." I twisted a piece of my auburn hair around my fingers.

"Were you the one who just called?"

I nodded.

"You got here fast, sweetie." She laughed. "We can definitely fit you in. If you'll just sign in down there." She gestured toward a clipboard on the edge of a small desk. "I'll get you going right after this."

"Thank you," I said, walking to the desk. Katie was

against the back wall, her hair clipped at odd angles as the plump brunette stood behind her, stirring her hair dye in a small, black bowl. "You know, actually, would you have time for some highlights?" I looked back at the woman—Carolyn, I guessed.

She squinted her eyes, glancing at the clock, then leaned her head to the side and yelled across the room. "What do you think, Tosh? Do you have time for highlights? What time's your next appointment?"

The brunette—Tosh—glanced at the clock, turning around to look at me. "Sure. As long as you don't mind that I rotate between you and Kat?" I shook my head. I didn't mind a bit. She jutted her head toward the chair, willing me to take a seat, but I wasn't looking. Instead, my eyes were locked on the woman in the chair. Katie...or, well, *Kat*. Her small, brown eyes were locked with mine in the reflection, her mouth tight with apparent displeasure. Obviously she wasn't in the mood to share hairdressers.

It was fine. I wasn't in the mood to share husbands.

I offered a small smile before making my way across the room and taking a seat in the salon chair directly beside Kat.

Tosh smiled at me. "I'm Toshia. Have you ever been here before?"

"Palmer," I told her, reaching out to shake her gloved hand. "And no. I haven't."

"New in town?"

"No, just...just in town for work," I said quickly.

Toshia didn't look convinced. She turned her attention back to start on Kat's hair, painting some of the bleach on her dark roots and wrapping them in foil.

"We don't get many people here for work, but I'm glad you stopped in. What are we going to do for you, Palmer?"

"I was thinking maybe just a few highlights. I...wanted a change." Kat was still staring at me, her eyes drilling holes in me through the reflection. Did she recognize me? Was she thinking I looked familiar? Had she stalked Ben's social media and seen his pictures of me? Heard my name? "I love that color," I told her.

"Thanks," Kat said softly, bobbing her head. She seemed to be a strange mix of annoyed and paralyzed by fear, and I couldn't deny that I felt the same, with just a dash of determination.

"Are you both...from here?" I asked.

Toshia nodded, with a quick laugh under her breath. "Born and raised. I've been doing Kat's hair since she was a baby."

"How nice."

"Where are you from, Palmer?" Kat asked, one brow raised slightly.

"I live in Oceanside."

"The big city, hm?" Toshia asked. "My husband and I love Oceanside. Do you know Sarah Allen? She's from there."

"No...I don't think I do." I played with my nails as Toshia continued to paint the highlights onto Kat's hair. It was mesmerizing, watching the white paste be smoothed over the dark roots. I tried to focus on that when it got to be too hard focusing on Kat's denial-filled gaze.

"I guess it's different there, hm? Everyone here knows everyone. Isn't that right, Kat?"

Kat nodded, glancing down at her phone. "Just about."

"What do you do, Kat?" I asked, trying to draw her attention back to me.

She shrugged a shoulder, not looking back up. "Nothing. My husband works."

Toshia blew air from her lips, popping her hip. "Oh, don't be so modest, Kat. Kat here's a successful food and travel blogger. They actually *pay* her to go on vacation. Can you believe that?"

Kat placed her phone in her lap and met Toshia's gaze, still avoiding mine at whatever cost. "Well, no one *pays* me to go on vacation. It's actually more of a free vacation for exposure on my blog. And...ads are where my income comes from. That's what I get paid for."

Toshia rolled her eyes. "Logistics. The point is...this girl's living the dream."

And trying to steal mine. "That sounds amazing. And you said you're married? What does your husband do?"

"He works on the railroad," came her clipped answer as she looked down.

Surprisingly, we had a connection there. "My uncle worked on the railroad. It's a hard job, but he loved it."

"He's away a lot," Toshia said. "He's on a job up in Canada right now. Next month could be Arizona or Illinois. He's always traveling. I worry about Kat all on her own, but the woman's fearless. Independent. She takes care of herself."

Fearless enough to steal my husband. Independent enough to cheat on hers. She takes care of herself by being selfish.

"What about you?" Kat asked, meeting my eye in the mirror again as Toshia unclipped the next layer of her hair. "What do you do...*Palmer*?" She said my name as though it was strange and foreign, and I couldn't help wondering again if she knew about me. Perhaps she did know who I was. My heart thudded in my chest as I became fearful I'd made a mistake going there. Following her. What if she managed to tip Ben off? What if they became sneakier with their affair?

"I do interior design and event planning with my best friend. We're working on opening our own firm. That's actually why I'm in town today, for work. I had to meet with a client here in Crestview, and he pushed our meeting back by a few hours. I figured rather than going back to the office and having to come back this afternoon, I'd just find something to do here in town."

"Event planning? Weddings and stuff?" Toshia asked. "My baby cousin's getting married next year. I'll have to send her your way."

"Oh, yeah, I'd love that. We do weddings, corporate parties, anniversaries, birthday parties, and everything in between. Weddings are my favorite." I beamed at her.

"Are you married?" Toshia asked, and I met Kat's pitiful gaze in the mirror once more.

"Yes. I am." I drew my words out, each syllable carrying weight.

"How long? What's his name?" Toshia asked, bobbing her head side to side, blissfully unaware of the tension between her clients.

"Just six months—" I froze as my phone began vibrating in my pocket. Did I detect a smile on Kat's lips? "Excuse me, I just have to take this." I stared at the screen with a sinking feeling. It was Ben. I considered not answering, but I'd never forgive myself if something had happened to Gray.

"Hello?" I asked, stepping away from the seat and out of the building in an instant.

"Where are you?" he asked.

"I'm…" There was no point in lying. Not if she'd already told him I was here, which is what I suspected. "I'm in Crestview."

His voice was shaking. "Crestview? Why?"

"I'm meeting with a client." *Keep your story straight, Palmer.* "Why? What's wrong?"

"Someone tried to break into the apartment, Palmer. Someone tried to break through the door. You need to get home."

His words sent ice through my veins. It was the absolute last thing I expected. "Wait…what?"

"Someone just tried to break into the apartment. I was in the bathroom giving Gray a bath. He'd had a blow out. Next thing I know, I hear someone beating on the door. I yelled 'Hang on!' but they just kept banging and banging. Then, it was like I could…I could hear wood splitting. I thought they were going to kill us. I just got so worried about what to do. I had no plan, no weapons…"

"Ben…calm down." I pulled my keys from my purse, running across the street. "You aren't making any sense. Why would someone want to break in? Did they get in? Did they break the door?"

"No. No. We're fine. Everything's fine, and they're gone. I wrapped Gray in a towel and ran into the living room, but before I could check who it was, they were gone. They must've had a crowbar or something. The wood trim by the lock is broken."

"It's the middle of the day. How is that even possible? Why would they try to break in midday?" We lived in a safe area. I'd never heard of any break-ins on our block, let alone in our building.

"I guess they assumed no one was home. I have no idea. Can you just get home please?" His voice was trembling as he spoke, and I could hear Gray crying in the background.

His cries brought me crashing into reality, suddenly terrified for his safety. What if they came back? What if I didn't make it in time? "Yes, of course. I'm on my way, okay? Oh my God. I just...I can't believe this. Call the police, Ben. Call the police, okay?"

"I will...just get home, okay? Please," he begged.

"I will. I'm on my way now." I ended the call and tossed my phone into the passenger's seat, trying and failing to get the key into the ignition thanks to my trembling fingers.

For the moment, Kat was forgotten. Nothing in the world mattered as much as getting home to protect my child. I'd do anything to protect him—no matter the enemy.

CHAPTER ELEVEN

Thirty minutes later, I arrived at the apartment. The door appeared to be in perfect shape, no damage, no dents. I pushed open the door, surprised to see it wasn't locked, and walked into my apartment. Gray was asleep in a bassinet in the middle of the room, and Ben was on the phone, leaning against the kitchen island.

I hurried to the bassinet, patting Gray's tummy gently. He cooed up at me, kicking his feet in the air, blissfully unaware that anything was wrong. Oh, to be that innocent again.

"Yeah, okay. Okay, thanks," Ben said, keeping his voice soft and low. "Sure thing. Okay. Bye." He hung up the phone, and I stared at him, unsure of what to say.

"Was that the police?"

"The super," he said, giving his head a sharp jerk.

"What did he say?"

"He's ordering a new piece of trim to go around the door." He pulled open the door and showed me the place where the tan trim had been torn back, splintering in several different directions. It was a small, rather unnoticeable amount of damage, but it was there. "But the deadbolt is still in place. There aren't any cameras or anything in the hallway, so there's not really anything he can do. He said we should make sure we have renters insurance and contact a security company."

"Well, that's helpful." I sighed.

"Most likely it was someone planning to break in while we were away, but when they heard me, they ran."

"Did they get any of the neighbors? What did the police say? Have there been any break-ins in this neighborhood recently? These things aren't usually random, right?"

He sighed. "Dimitri said calling the police wouldn't get us far. We wouldn't even be a priority with just a piece of trim broken. What do you think? Should I call? It doesn't look like any of the other apartments were bothered."

My jaw dropped open. "Of course you should call, Ben. They'll have to do a report. Why haven't you already called? You should've done that first."

"I called Dimitri first to see about getting a copy of the security tape in case the police needed it, and to let him know it happened. He just said it's up to us, but that in his experience, it's best not to bother with the police for something like this."

"There's a security camera at the front entrance, right?" I asked, thinking back. This was supposed to be a safe neighborhood. We'd never had any issues before. It was why I'd chosen to live here alone before Ben. I'd always felt safe.

"Yeah, it doesn't work, apparently. I'll do whatever you

think's best. I just don't want the police to think we're wasting their time when nothing even happened. You know what they say, even filing a report when something *was* stolen, you're not likely to get it back. So filing one when nothing was stolen seems silly to me."

"But they broke our trim, so they obviously wanted in for some reason. What happens next time when no one's home?"

"I'll call if you want me to. If it'll make you feel more comfortable. Do you want me to?"

I chewed my bottom lip. I wanted him to call, yes. I wanted justice. I wanted answers. But, at the same time, I knew he was right. There was likely very little that would be done or even *could* be done. "Dimitri really wasn't worried about it?"

He glanced at his phone. "He said he can get some trim, so there's no reason to file an insurance claim, and with nothing else damaged or missing, the cops won't take us seriously."

"Okay." I paused, unable to deny the worry in my belly. I needed to do the right thing, to keep my child safe. "No, I'm sorry. I hear what you're saying, but I want you to call. Even if they don't take us seriously, I want them to have it on record that this happened."

"Okay," Ben said, nodding slowly. He picked up his phone. "I'll call."

THE POLICE MADE it a *top priority* and arrived to take our report just over three hours later. Right from the start, I could tell Ben had been right. It was a mistake to call.

The officers who came, Officers Hendricks and Malone, made a big show of examining the door and the torn trim before they entered our apartment, listening to Ben as he went over the day's events.

"This is an old building, lots of scuffs on the walls. Are you sure the trim was damaged because of this? Sometimes you just don't notice damage until you really examine it."

Ben was tight-lipped, already irritated that I'd pushed the call. "It wasn't damaged before. We would've noticed."

"Okay, so," he flipped open a notepad, though he didn't produce a pen, "do you have any reason to be worried that someone might break in? Did you recently make any large purchases, sit boxes on the curb? Do you have any enemies?"

"We haven't made any large purchases, and our trash goes in the bin around back. It's a shared dumpster for the whole complex. And, no, to my knowledge, we have no enemies." He glanced at me for a half-second, irritation emanating from him.

"What about you?" Hendricks asked. "Any enemies? Anything suspicious?"

I shook my head. "This has always been a quiet neighborhood. We've never had issues, even with packages being left at our doors. They've always been left alone."

"Are there any new neighbors?" he asked, finally pulling a pen from his pocket. "Anyone who could've brought trouble?"

"Not that I've seen," I said. "Ben's home during the day, though." I looked at him.

"I haven't seen anyone new, no. We were lucky to get this place. The building is sought after. Palmer had been on the waiting list for a year before she moved in. Once people get here, they tend to stay."

He jotted something down in a notebook. "Does your property manager live on site? We'll want to check with them. I didn't notice any cameras in the hall... Do they have them?"

He was asking questions as fast as we could answer them, obviously not too concerned about what we were saying. The other officer stood silently around him, his eyes traveling around the room. "Dimitri's our super. I can give you his number. He lives downstairs. Next to the office. And, no, there aren't any cameras. The ones outside don't work."

"Well, that's useful." Hendricks smirked.

"We had no idea until today," I said.

At the same time Ben said, "We didn't exactly install them ourselves."

"Right," Hendricks said, and I winced as he closed his notebook. He already wasn't taking us seriously, and my husband's attitude wasn't helping. "Well, we can dust for prints, but I have to be honest with you. In a building this size, prints are going to be all over the place, and if the perp just knocked and never touched the door, aside from whatever he may have used to try to pry the door open, he most likely didn't touch anything. There's a good chance his prints aren't here at all." He nodded to Malone, who immediately got to work. "Do you have a security system installed?"

"No," I said, casting my eyes to the ground.

He inhaled, directing the rest of the conversation directly at me. "Well, I'd suggest you get one. If this guy does come back, it's better to be safe than sorry."

CHAPTER TWELVE

"It's so good to see you, Palmer," Ty said, his dark skin crinkling around his eyes as he smiled and pulled me into a hug. I reached for Dannika next. "I'm sorry Ben and Gray couldn't come. I was hoping to meet your little guy finally. Dannika just raves about him."

It had been more than a month since our last double date with Dannika and her husband, Ty, and I couldn't help feeling sad that I'd had to lie about the pretenses for needing to see them as well as why Ben couldn't join us.

Ty pulled Dannika's seat out, letting her sit before he did. "Yeah, he wanted to be here. He just had some errands he had to take care of this morning. Life as a stay-at-home dad doesn't leave much room for free time."

Ty's brow shot up. "I'd imagine so, and I can't say I envy him."

The waitress approached our table and took our orders. When she left, we carried on.

"I think he enjoys it, actually, and I can't say I'm not a

little jealous myself." I unfolded my napkin and placed it in my lap.

Ty leaned back in his chair with a deep, warm chuckle. "Wait 'til you have three. Trust us, you'll be aching for a chance to get to work."

Dannika nodded in agreement, casting a joy-filled glance at her husband. "She doesn't know about that yet. You just let them enjoy the fun honeymoon phase while it lasts." She patted his chest lovingly.

Ty lifted his fingers from the table, keeping his wrist in place. "Fair enough. Just, like she said, enjoy it while it lasts because it *does not.*"

I laughed. "How are things at the firm, Ty?"

Having my best friend's husband be a divorce attorney hadn't been planned, but using it to my advantage was definitely a perk.

"Well, like I said, that honeymoon phase doesn't last, and that just happens to make me a whole lot of money." His eyes grew wide with pleasure as he spoke, his thin, black mustache bouncing with each word. "We've been busier than usual even, I think it's the summer heat, but I can't complain." He elbowed Dannika. "Even if I wanted to, she wouldn't let me."

"I told him about your big client, Palmer. About what it could mean for us," Dannika said, her teeth bared with hope.

"Dani's been bragging on you. I know how hard you've both worked to get where you are. It sounds like you'll be ready to open up shop soon, huh?"

"That's the hope," I said, taking a deep breath. "I'm always the cautious one, especially with Gray now."

"Hey, I get it," he said, his expression serious. "It took me years to pull the trigger on going out on my own. Dani was always the one pushing me to do it."

"And I was right, wasn't I?" she asked, lips pursed. "Just like I'll be right this time."

"Yeah, you were. You're always right." He leaned over, pressing his lips to hers. When they broke apart, the waitress appeared with our food and drinks. Ty leaned back, letting her place Dannika's plate in front of her, then Ty's, and finally mine. We were stark opposites: Dannika and Ty with their salmon and salad and me with my BLT and fries. I really should've attempted to learn some good habits from them.

"So, I have a question." I popped a fry in my mouth, trying to appear more casual than I felt. My hands were shaking, and I hoped he wouldn't notice. I'd been rehearsing the question all morning, trying to decide the best way to bring it up. Best case, he'd ask me if I was considering divorce randomly, as a sales pitch, which of course didn't happen. So we were going with the worst case now.

"What's that?" Dannika asked, already cutting into her meat.

"It's for Ty, actually. A friend of mine is…well, she's considering getting a divorce. I was wondering if I could get some free legal advice for her?" I winced.

He took a bite, a closed-mouth grin growing on his lips. When he swallowed, he said, "Sure thing. Whatcha got?"

"Who's the friend?" Dannika asked as she popped a bite into her mouth. "Anyone I know?"

"Just someone I went to school with," I said, probably too quickly. "You don't know her."

She nodded, taking another bite of her food and looking at Ty, who was looking at me.

"She thinks her husband could be cheating on her," I said.

"Oh, no," Dannika said, her voice low.

"Yeah, but, I mean, she doesn't have a ton of money, but the money they do have is hers. It was hers before they met. A savings account and a few CDs. She doesn't want to leave him if it will mean splitting everything." I paused, watching his expression, which turned serious rather quickly.

"Well, as far as the marital estate, there's not much that can be done unless there was a prenup in place. But, alimony...alimony can be affected by an affair, if there's irrefutable proof an affair occurred. Does she have proof? You said she thinks he could be cheating... She doesn't know for sure?"

I shook my head, letting what he'd said wash over me. If I were to leave Ben, half of what I'd worked for, sacrificed for my whole life, would legally belong to him. All because he'd cheated on me. I tried to keep the heartbreak from being too evident on my expression, though I doubted I was doing very well. "No, she doesn't know for sure. She's caught him with a woman, lying about where he was, but she still hasn't found proof that anything happened between them. They met in public."

He inhaled through his shimmery, white teeth. "See, that's where she needs to start. Has she brought up the affair to him yet? Does he know she's suspicious? If he lied to her about it, I guess so…"

"Well, no. He doesn't know. At least, not as far as I know. She asked him where he was and he lied, but she didn't confront him about it."

He took another bite, chewing thoughtfully. "Your friend's a smart girl. My advice would be, before she says or does anything, she needs to get proof. Cell phone records, bank records, photos, video…whatever she can get. The more evidence she could present to a judge, the better. Then, once she has what she thinks is enough, she should talk to a lawyer, make sure the case is solid, before she serves him with the papers. Did you give her my number?"

Dannika was watching me closely, and I felt my face warming under her scrutiny. "I haven't yet. Do you have a business card?"

"Sure thing," he said, pulling a business card carrier from his pocket on demand. He slid a card to me across the table. "Tell her to give me a call before she does anything rash. Even if I can just answer some questions."

"Thank you," I said, placing the card into my purse in the seat next to me. "You're the best, Ty."

He grinned. "I'm happy to help. Plus Dannika'd kill me if I didn't." He winked.

"No, I wouldn't," she said, her lips pressed together as sarcasm hung on her words. "I'd need you to get me off the murder trial."

"I don't do criminal trials, so you'd be out of luck, but fair enough," Ty said as I giggled. They'd been married eighteen years, had three beautiful children and a lifetime of stories, and still, they were perfect. All I'd ever wanted was to have something like they did. When I'd met Ben, I was sure I'd found it. But apparently I'd been wrong. *Again*. I was starting to think I'd never have what they did. Maybe I wasn't worthy of that forever kind of love after all. It seemed so few people were lucky enough to get it.

"You okay, Palmer?" Dannika asked, and I realized my vision had begun to blur with tears.

I dusted them away quickly, forcing a warm smile. "I'm fine. Just my allergies."

She nodded, still watching me closely. It was uncomfortable the way she was locked into me, but I couldn't blame her. She knew me better than anyone. Which meant, try as I might to deny it, she knew when I was lying.

CHAPTER THIRTEEN

The next day, the phone rang from the cupholder of my car, and I glanced down. *The office.* I knew who it was and why she was calling. Unlike Cumberland, and even Howie to some extent, Dannika wasn't buying my lies about going to client meetings. She knew how I worked, and she knew something was up. But I couldn't tell her. Couldn't explain to her what was going on when I still had no idea myself.

I pressed the volume button, silencing it, and stared into the large, glass windows of the restaurant. It was raining outside, which I hoped would mean Ben would choose to stay home. Instead, just thirty minutes after I left the house, he departed from the building with Gray in his arms. This time, instead of walking toward the park, they walked around the building and, for a brief moment, I lost sight of them. Just as I started the car and made my way back down the street, his car pulled out. I froze, panicked that he'd see me, but he didn't seem to. Instead, he pulled out like normal and headed in the opposite direction. I stayed a car or two behind him, turning down separate streets and keeping a safe distance, but never losing sight of him completely.

He got on the interstate, headed toward Crestview, and I felt the last bit of hope collapse inside of me. I'd thought—hoped—he'd be going anywhere else, but he wasn't. He was going to see her again. Finally, all my suspicions were confirmed. This was real. It was really happening.

He surprised me by taking an exit that was still a few miles shy of Crestview and pulling into a restaurant parking lot on the outskirts of Oceanside.

I pulled into a parking garage, inserting seven dollars in cash from my wallet, and took a spot near the edge. I climbed from the car and stepped in front of the hood, looking out over the waist-high concrete partition. I could see into the restaurant across the street, where Ben and Gray had taken a table near the window. He was holding Gray against his chest, my son sleeping in his arms, and he watched out the window. Watched for her.

Fifteen minutes after they arrived, Kat showed up. With each click of her heels across the concrete, inaudible from where I stood so many feet up, yet painful just the same, I felt my anger growing. Ben was smiling when she walked in the restaurant, and he turned his back to me as I watched her approach him.

She sat down in the booth next to him, their skin touching. It was killing me. My insides bubbled with anger and fear. How long would it take him to leave me?

How long had he been seeing her in the first place? How dare she? How dare he? Would she tell him about seeing me at the salon? Did she even know me? She had to know he had a wife. He had a son, for crying out loud. Had he killed me off in some fantasy life with her?

I felt tears prick my eyes, but brushed them away, holding my phone up and snapping a picture of the two of them. I clicked on the lower left screen, pulling up the photo.

From this far away, the picture was blurry, misshapen, and dark from the glare on the glass. It would never work. I needed to get down to their level. Get closer. But I couldn't chance them seeing me. The warning Ty had given rang through my head. I had to get proof before he found out I knew. I had to.

I stood, leaning against the concrete as I stared down at my husband, child, and the stranger, feeling sick. I wanted to walk away, I was no use to anyone standing there, but I couldn't make myself move. I wanted to take my son away from him. How dare he bring him, the child I'd just had ripped from my womb, and share him with someone else? He was mine. *Mine.*

I snapped another, albeit blurry, photo of the three of them together, her practically hanging off his arm as she stared down at my son. One way or another, I was going to fix this. For me. For Gray.

My teeth ground down so hard I winced, releasing the tension. The waitress approached their table and took their orders. I could see the way she was looking at them, as if they were the perfect family.

To unknowing eyes, I knew that's what they looked like.

To mine, they were a family destined to be torn apart. And mine would be the hands to do the tearing.

CHAPTER FOURTEEN

B en surprised me by staying at the restaurant well past lunch, well past the time that their table was cleared and the waitress had gone from enchanted to annoyed.

When they finally decided to leave, separating from each other and walking in opposite directions, I slipped my phone back into my pocket. I'd taken three photos, all blurry, during their dinner. I couldn't take them to Ty. It was embarrassing enough having to go to him at all. I couldn't bring him photos that were so pixelated and grainy you couldn't tell who they were or what was happening in them.

Ben pulled out, though rather than turning left, he turned right, then right again. We were going in the opposite direction of home. *Why?*

He took the turn onto the interstate, and I hung back, waiting until they were several cars ahead of me to follow him. He was heading to Crestview. Even before I knew it, I knew.

I should've stopped him. Called him and told him I knew everything, but if I wanted this to work, I couldn't. If he was going to be entitled to half my life savings, when he'd come into the marriage with none, I was going to make sure he wasn't entitled to alimony. And to do that, as sick as it made me, I had to let it play out.

Kat's car was nowhere in sight. He wasn't following her. *He knows the way to her house without following her. He's been there enough that he has it memorized.* The realization struck me, and that fact, more than anything else, broke my heart. He'd been there before. How many times? While I was pregnant? While I was dealing with morning sickness and mood swings and an unbearable fear of what I was doing, was he coming to Crestview to see his mistress? Was he pretending I didn't exist when he was with her?

I batted back tears, turning onto the Crestview exit after he did. He turned right, rather than left, and I grew hopeful for a second. Maybe I'd been wrong.

Eventually, though, he pulled into the drive of the familiar house and climbed from the car just as I made a lap. For fear he'd see my car and recognize it, I parked this time in front of the house behind hers, on a completely separate street. The driveway was empty, lights off. No signs of life.

I climbed from the car and rushed across the road, darting through the yard of the empty house. From their backyard, I could clearly see into Kat's. I stared at the tree house where I'd hidden before. I'd have to be even more careful this time, especially with Ben there. I'd been so lucky last time, but that may not be the case anymore.

I stepped into her backyard, hurrying across the ankle-high grass and toward the tree. I launched myself onto it, placing a foot on the first rung, when I heard the back door open. My stomach hurt from the sudden burst of movement, but I had to keep moving.

Shoot.

Shoot.

Shoot.

Shoot.

I climbed the ladder quickly, keeping my arms and legs as close together as possible to avoid sticking out behind the width of the tree. I shoved myself up, laying flat on the floor of the tree house with a pounding heart and ice-cold veins. Who was it? Who was coming? Had they seen me?

I didn't dare lift my head, too afraid of who'd be looking back at me.

"That's better, isn't it, little guy?" I heard her ask. I lifted my head on instinct. To my great relief, they weren't looking for me and hadn't discovered me. I shifted my weight, sliding my legs against the wooden floor until I was in a crouched position. I pushed up, moving a millimeter a second as I inched my way across the tree house and toward the window.

Once I'd reached it, I lifted up, staring down at the scene below. Ben and Kat were sitting on her patio, Gray resting peacefully in her arms. It stung. Worse than Ben betraying me, Gray had done so, too. I knew it wasn't rational, but that's how it felt. Seeing him so close to her, his little fist gripping the fabric of her shirt, it was enough to make me sick. I couldn't stop the hot, angry tears from falling as I watched them together.

"He likes you," Ben said, cocking his head to the side to look at her. My hands balled into fists.

"Of course he does," Kat said. "Everyone likes me." *Not everyone, I assure you.* "Oh, Ben, he's so perfect."

I could hear the smile in his voice, despite not being able to see it. "I think he's pretty great, too." He sighed, leaning back and resting his arms behind his head. He glanced up at the tree house, and I shot down, breathing heavily. *Did he see me?* "He'd love growing up in a place like this."

"I wish he could," she said sadly. "I always dreamed of my kids playing in this yard. In my old tree house."

They were silent, and I didn't dare stand back up. My heart thudded so loudly I was sure they could hear it. A spider crawled across the board above my hand, and I jerked it back, suppressing a scream. Down below, Gray began to fuss.

"Oh, no, sweet boy. Don't cry. Momma's here."

My stomach tensed at her words, and I had to squeeze the board in front of me to keep from launching from the tree house, Spiderman-style. I couldn't stop myself from looking back out the window, where Kat could be seen, lowering the edge of her shirt for my son and placing him to her breast.

No.

I saw red, my vision blurry with rage as I fought back bile and tried to rein in my fury.

I wanted to kill her.

I wanted to kill him.

I looked at Ben, who, to my relief, looked concerned.

"Oh, I don't know if you should…"

"It's fine, Ben," she said, smiling down as my son struggled to latch onto her breast. "See, he's hungry. It's calming him."

"I don't want to confuse him, Kat. I have some milk in the bag I can warm up for him," he said. "Just wait a second." He stood and darted in the house, leaving just the three of us there. Just me, Kat, and Gray. I wanted to jump down, to grab Gray from her arms and run for the hills, but I couldn't. I was angry enough that I could do something stupid if I wasn't careful. I was trespassing. This could all be misconstrued. I could be arrested, I could lose Gray anyway. I had to be smart. I had to, no matter how high the bile rose in my throat or how much I trembled with pure rage.

Gray wasn't latching on. She wasn't me. He struggled to attach to her, and she didn't know how to place him right. Even if she would've done everything perfectly, there was no milk in her breasts like there was in mine. No nourishment for the child in her arms. She wasn't his mother.

"Come on, sweet boy," she said, pushing his head against her body a bit more firmly. I chewed my lip, my options getting fewer and fewer by the moment. I was going to have to intervene. I was going to end up going to jail over this.

No sooner had I accepted my decision than the back door opened again and Ben appeared with a bottle, half-full of my milk. "Here we go," he said. I expected Kat to argue, and from the look on her face, I believed she wanted to, but after a moment, she lowered Gray from her chest, pulling her shirt up over her bare breast—not before giving my husband an eyeful—and reaching her hand out for the bottle. She rested Gray in one arm and held the bottle to his lips, and his fussing stopped almost instantly.

He was calmed by *me*. By something my body produced. It was the only thing keeping me still in a moment where I was sure I'd come unglued. I watched him sucking the milk down and breathed in heavily, out slowly. I felt the hairs on my arms stand up, my body tense. I was nearing a panic attack, but I couldn't let it happen here.

I had to breathe.

That was all.

I just had to keep breathing.

No. An angry thought hit me at once. I'd missed my chance. I should've taken a picture of what was happening. Of her attempting to nurse my son while my husband allowed it. Surely that would've helped my case. But it was too late. The moment had passed, and I'd been too distracted by fury to catch it.

I sank to the floor in a state of panic as the adrenaline I'd felt began to calm down. I tried to keep my breathing steady, to keep myself quiet as I felt the sobs beating against my chest, begging to be released. The hair on my arms stood on end as I pressed my hand to my lips so hard, my teeth hurt.

Just breathe, Palmer.

Just breathe.

CHAPTER FIFTEEN

I went back to work without thinking about it. It was the last thing I wanted to do, and yet I also didn't want to go home. I sat in the parking lot for an hour, crying and snotting and fuming.

How had it come to this?

How had so much gone so wrong this quickly?

How had I fallen from perfect wife, loving mother to wife betrayed in a matter of days? It didn't seem possible. And yet, here I was. Again. Why was I so easy to cheat on? Why was I so easy to lose?

I wiped away my tears, lowering the sun visor and opening the mirror to look over my makeup. My hair had frizzed from the humidity, most of my makeup melting away, and I had tear stains on the makeup that had fought to remain.

I couldn't go into my building like this, but I couldn't go home. I couldn't face the conversation that I needed to have. Ty had advised that I wait until I had proof, but there was absolutely no way I could face Ben without telling him what I knew, what I'd seen, and how I felt.

He left Kat's house just before I did, so he should've been home by now. I pulled out my phone and typed up a quick, emotionless text.

Hey. What are you up to?

He'd lie and pretend he wasn't doing anything wrong. Pretend he and Gray had spent the morning at home, as usual. He'd lie like he always had. Because I was the kind of woman who men lied to. I was the kind of woman they cheated on. The kind who was easily replaced. The kind you traded in for a new model after a while.

Two completely different men in two completely different scenarios had cheated on me. The only common denominator was me. I had to believe that meant something.

I ran a hand over my belly, several pounds of extra fluff still lingering since I'd had Gray. I knew some women who lost the baby weight almost instantly, but I still carried at least twenty pounds extra. My breasts were swollen and sore, and they belonged solely to Gray now. I wore thick, diaper-like pads in my hinged nursing bra to keep the milk from leaking through my clothes. I had several more weeks of bleeding before Ben and I could be intimate again. Not that he'd want to. I was no longer the sexy, enchanting woman he had met a year ago. Could I really blame him for falling in love with someone else? We'd been together such a short time before I'd fallen pregnant and he'd proposed. Maybe he felt like I'd trapped him. Maybe I had.

Fat tears fell down my cheeks as I waited for his return

text. I needed to pump. I needed to eat. I needed to wash my face and change my clothes. I put the car in drive and pulled out of the parking lot, heading across town to deal with the shambles that appeared to be all that remained of my life.

I PARKED the car and stepped into the building with determination. I would hear Ben out, but I wouldn't back down. What he'd done was wrong. What he'd allowed Kat to do was beyond wrong. I wouldn't forgive him for it. If he wanted to be with her—if he wanted to leave me—I wouldn't beg him to stay, but he had to know I wouldn't walk away with my tail tucked. I'd fight for custody. Fight against alimony.

As I climbed the stairs, a sick thought filled my mind. Now that Ben was home full time, what if he could get custody more easily? What if I'd set him up to receive alimony without even realizing it? Women did it all the time in divorces, didn't they? It may be no different here.

I shoved the thought out of my head. It wasn't going to happen like that. Ty was the best of the best, and I had him on my side of this. Whoever Ben hired wouldn't be nearly as good as who I had on my side.

I approached the door and put my hand on the knob, twisting it carefully. It was locked. I lowered my brows, knocking. Why was it locked?

After a moment, I groaned and dug through my purse, locating my keys and unlocking the door.

"Ben?"

The first thing I noticed was the silence. It was deafening when I was so used to hearing life coming from the apartment. Gray fussing. Ben tapping his feet. Ben laughing. Gray cooing. There was nothing this time.

"Ben?" I called again, keeping my voice low, though a worried feeling had settled low in my stomach. *Something is wrong.*

I walked down the hall with caution, my footsteps the only sound I could hear. The humidity from an impending storm had settled into the apartment in such a short time, and a bead of sweat gathered on my upper lip. "Ben? Where are you?" I called once more as I stepped into the bedroom. The room, like the rest of the apartment, was empty and silent. My husband and son were nowhere to be found.

I pulled out my phone and clicked on his name from my recent calls list. It didn't ring.

"Hey, it's Ben. Leave me a message, and I'll get back to you."

The line beeped, and I hung up. *Where is he?*

I walked back into the living room, searching the place for any sign of a note from him explaining his disappearance. When I'd left Kat's house, he was gone. It wasn't possible that he hadn't made it home yet if this was where he was headed.

There were no papers, no notes, nothing out of place. The stroller still sat against the wall, so despite the fact that the rain wasn't here yet, it was doubtful that he'd taken him on a walk. I had a sinking feeling of dread that I couldn't explain. Everything in me screamed that something was very wrong.

I opened the apartment door, locking it behind me and jogging down the stairs. I glanced out at the street, thankful that the rain had held off. I searched the street, looking for signs of his car to no avail, then turned the corner to head around the building. I looked throughout the small parking lot and inside the underground parking garage, hurrying through each level in search of the silver Mazda. It wasn't there. He wasn't there.

Once I'd reached the last level of the garage, I turned back around. I walked up the sidewalk back to my apartment slowly, watching for his car, just hoping it would appear.

Where are you, Ben?

I had such a bad feeling. But how could I explain it? And what was I supposed to do with it, anyway? How was I supposed to fix it? How was I going to find them? I called my office first, on a whim.

"Thank you for calling Cumberland Design, Palmer Lewis' office. How may I help you?"

"Howie, it's me," I said, letting out a huff.

"Palmer? Hey! Are you still in Spring Hill?"

I shook my head, though he couldn't see me. "No. I…" I had no reason to lie to him, but I needed to. Howie had more than earned my trust, but I couldn't explain to him everything that was going on. I didn't have the energy. "I just dropped by the apartment to eat lunch. Listen, Ben and Gray didn't happen to come there, did they?"

He paused. "You mean today? I haven't seen them. Were they supposed to?" His voice grew faint, and I could tell he was leaning away from the receiver, careening his neck around the office to get a good look. I could picture it well.

"No, I just...they aren't here, and he's not answering his phone." I chewed my bottom lip. "They'll turn up. I just wanted to make sure I hadn't missed him."

"They aren't here, but if they do show up, I'll have him call you."

"Thanks, Howie," I said.

"Will you be back in—"

I'd already lowered my phone, and I couldn't bear to worry about the answer to that question. There was still so much unknown. I needed to call someone else —but who?

I didn't have the phone numbers of any of the men he used to work with. I could call the store, but why would they be there? I clicked on his name again, but still, it went straight to voicemail. Had his phone died? Worse, had he turned it off?

I tried to fight back the worry and the fear that ricocheted through every inch of my body, wrapping its spider-like fingers around my organs, telling me to do something—anything—to make this better. I had no idea what to do. No idea how to make this any better. How could I be this helpless?

Ben had no relationship with his family, so I didn't have much more than their names. No phone numbers, no addresses even, other than the knowledge that they lived out of state, and just getting that much was like prying teeth from my husband.

You try looking up Mark and Kathy Lewis and let me know how far you get.

I opened the freezer and gasped. All of Gray's milk was gone. Every single bag. More than a week's worth. Had he brought all of that to Kat's? I hadn't seen how much he had packed.

I didn't want to drive back to Crestview, especially for no reason, but I was out of options. My keys were still in my hand, purse around my shoulder, as if somehow, I'd just known that this would happen. I'd known I'd have to leave. Have to go after them.

I pulled open the door and stopped. My head was so fuzzy with fear I couldn't really concentrate. He hadn't mentioned going anywhere, had he? I didn't think so.

I sucked in a breath, locking the door behind me and rushing down the stairs, switching my phone's ringer to loud. The rain pelted me—*why wouldn't it decide to start now, of all times?*—the wind blowing my hair and my clothes wildly as I made my way to the car.

Please call me back.

CHAPTER SIXTEEN

I drove with ferocity through the raging storm that had
blown in suddenly, heading for Kat's house with no
regard for speed limits or traffic laws. I could think of
nothing more than the image of my son's head settling
onto her chest. Why had Ben left? Why wasn't he home?
Where was my child?

I pulled up in front of the small, white cottage,
surprised to see an unfamiliar vehicle in the drive. A man
wearing a sweat-soaked red T-shirt stepped through the
front door of the house, wiping his forehead with the
back of his hand. He was holding a phone to his ear with
the opposite hand.

I hesitated, checking the street again. I was at the right
house, so who was this?

I caught the glint of a wedding band around his finger.
This is her husband.

She'd mentioned he worked out of town, but he
must've returned home. How was I going to explain who I
was? Why I was there? Kat's car wasn't in the driveway.

He stared at me with a furrowed brow, not speaking as I stepped from the car getting pelted by the rain, and I stared back, keeping the door open. Did he know who I was? What I knew? "Hey, let me call you back. I love you, too." He lowered the phone from his ear. "Can I help you?"

"Is…is Kat here?" I asked, my voice quivering with nerves and adrenaline.

"No," he said, his tone clipped. "Who're you?"

"I'm…" *A friend? An enemy? Her boyfriend's wife?* "I'm looking for Ben Lewis. Do you know him or…?"

He shook his head, no recognition, worry, or anger in his expression. I'd one-upped him. I'd caught them when he still knew nothing of what was going on. No idea that his wife was betraying him. I stared at the ring on his finger again. He had no idea it was coming. I didn't feel triumphant—I felt sick. I should have told him, but I didn't have the energy.

He opened the door again, standing halfway over the threshold to let me know he was done with the conversation and preparing to go back inside.

"Do you—sorry, do you know when Kat'll be back? Or where I could find her?"

He shook his head again, watching me closely. "Are you a friend of hers or something?"

"Not exactly…" I wasn't sure what to say, how to explain it.

"Wanna leave your name? I can make sure she knows you stopped by."

"No, that's…that's okay. I'll come back."

He pressed his lips together without another word.

"Okay, well, thank you." I sank back down into the car,

already soaked to the bone from the storm. He didn't acknowledge me as he walked back into his house, and I started the car again.

Where are you, Ben?

I knew he had to be with Kat. There was no question. But her husband coming home threw a wrench in my theories. Had he come home early? Had she known he'd be returning? What if he'd found out and done something to Ben? But Ben was gone when I left, so that made no sense.

I drove back home, wishing the rain would let up just a bit. My windshield wipers zipped across the glass feverishly, working to clear up the blurry windshield. I drove slowly, unable to see the lines in the road. The storm was bad, but it was no match for the storm raging inside me.

I stopped by the restaurant I'd watched them at earlier that day and then checked Gary's Grill in case they'd returned there, but they were nowhere to be found.

It was as if they'd disappeared entirely.

I headed back to the apartment with fresh panic in my chest, each breath tighter than the last. Where could they be? What should I do next?

I pulled up to the apartment, checking the street and parking lot for Ben's car. It wasn't there. I walked inside quickly, using my hands as a makeshift umbrella, wracking my brain for where they might be, where I hadn't thought to check.

Ice-cold fear hit me with a vengeance. *The storm.* What if they'd been in an accident? *Should I check the hospital?* What if something happened?

I pulled up Google in my browser as I climbed the stairs, searching for our local hospital's phone number and pressing the phone to my ear when it began to ring.

"Saint Francis Medical."

"Hi, um, I…I wanted to check and see if my husband and son were brought there. I can't find them at home, and I'm worried they've been in an accident."

The woman's voice quickly changed from apathetic to concerned. "Of course. Can I have their names and descriptions please? Would your husband have been traveling with an ID?"

"Yes, he would've had his wallet on him. His name's Ben Lewis. He's got brown hair and a slim build. A tattoo of a compass on his right wrist. And he had my son with him, Gray. He's just over two weeks old with reddish-brown hair and blue eyes."

"Let me place you on hold just a moment, okay? Bear with me."

I gripped the phone tighter, my palms slick with rain and sweat. "Okay, sure."

Classical music rang out over the line, and I walked through my front door, looking around to be sure they hadn't come home during my absence, but as I expected, they were nowhere to be found.

"Ma'am?" She came back to me as I ran a finger across our countertop. "Are you still there?"

"Yes, yes, I'm here." *Please have them. Please let them be okay.* I held my breath.

"We don't have anyone here that matches the descriptions you provided."

"Okay." I wasn't sure how to feel—happy because they weren't in the hospital, or worried because that meant I still had no idea where they might be.

"You might try Western Baptist if you still aren't able to contact them," she offered. "I hope you find them safe."

"Thank you," I whispered, pulling the phone from my ear and ending the call. Back to square one. I walked to my couch and sat down, every inch of my skin crawling with worry. I wanted to call the police, but I had no idea what to say. No idea if I was overreacting. I dialed Ben's number again and was immediately sent to voicemail.

Where are you, Ben?

Where are you, Gray baby?

Crestview didn't have a hospital, and the only other one in Oceanside was on the north side of town. It would've been out of the way if they'd had an accident between here and Crestview. I Googled the non-emergency line for our police department, staring at the ten digits with apprehension. I didn't want to do this. I didn't want them to think I was overreacting.

But I had to. I had to know what was happening.

I connected the call and followed the prompts until I was able to speak to a live person.

"Yes, hi. Um, my husband and my son are…missing, I think. I'm not really sure what to do."

"Okay, well, what do you mean you *think* they're missing?"

I brushed away the tears as they came, my voice cracking with each word I spoke. I just wanted them to walk through the front door. I just wanted it to have all been a misunderstanding. "I came home from work, and they aren't here. I can't get a hold of my husband. I've already checked local hospitals."

"Okay, let me transfer you to one of our officers. Please hold."

AN HOUR LATER, the police were in my apartment, dripping wet. They walked through the apartment, checking over it with a fine-toothed comb. Once they'd done that, they returned to me.

The first officer, Officer Kessler, was friendly but professional, her long black hair tied back in a tight bun. She sat me down on the couch, as her partner, Officer McGuire, did the same. I was having trouble focusing on what she was saying while my mind was listening carefully to every bump outside in the hallway. I just wanted him to come home. "Okay, so we're going to get through this the best we can. I know it's an emotional time, and I know you're scared. We're going to do everything we can to find your family, Mrs. Lewis, okay? First, we just need to get some information so we can get an idea of where to start. What can you tell us about your husband? Was it usual for him to go anywhere during the day? Does he have any places he frequents? Have you checked with his friends?" She held unrelenting eye contact with me as she fired the questions at me.

I sniffed, running a finger under my nose. *Where are you, Gray baby?* Why weren't they doing anything? Why weren't they searching? Why were we still sitting here? "He…he doesn't really have friends. There are a few guys he used to work with, but they didn't…you know, hang out, really. Not since he left work. He began staying home when we had our son—"

"And you mentioned on the phone your son is just a few weeks old, right?"

I nodded, my voice catching in my throat as my chest grew tight. He was going to be turning three weeks old. I'd see him again before that happened, right? I had to. "That's right. He's just shy of three weeks old now."

"Okay, great, go on." As we spoke, Officer McGuire took notes from behind her, his eyes quietly wandering the room, expression solemn.

"Well, he doesn't really have friends or anything, is what I'm saying. He hadn't told me about any plans for today and, even if he'd planned to do something, there's no reason for his phone to be off." There was no reason for him to take my son away from me for any length of time. He knew how attached I was to Gray. He knew how much I needed him home with me.

She pressed her lips together. "Were there any issues between the two of you? You were newly married, is that right?"

I tried not to let her question offend me, but I dreaded telling her what I'd have to next. "We are. We've been married just over six months." I let her piece together what that meant. Yes, we'd gotten married after we found out about Gray, but that didn't change anything. Ben and I were happy, or so I'd thought. We loved Gray more than anything, I knew. That baby was the best thing to ever happen to me. To us. "But things have been fine. We argue over little things, of course, but nothing major."

"Do you have any recent pictures of Ben and Gray? And I'll need to know what they were wearing last."

"Of course," I said, rushing across the room and lifting the photo frame from the end table with myself and Ben. I could hardly look down at the photo without bursting into tears. Then I walked toward the pile of papers still on the counter from our hospital stay, searching for Gray's hospital photos. I pulled one from the folder and carried them back to the officer, tracing a finger over his tiny features. *Come back to me, sweet boy.* "Here you go."

She looked them over carefully. "Thank you for these. It's okay that we keep them?"

"Of course." *Just bring me my son back.*

She passed them to McGuire. "And can you tell me what they were wearing when you last saw them?"

"Right," I said, remembering she'd already asked me that. I tried to picture Gray, the last time I'd seen him without crying. It was nearly impossible. "Um, well...I believe Ben was wearing khaki shorts and a light blue T-shirt. Gray was dressed in a white onesie and blue jeans." I breathed slowly, trying to make sure she could understand me through the sobs. She was gracious, letting me cry as much as I needed, while still moving the interview along.

"And that was this morning, correct? What time did you leave for work?"

I chewed my lip, sniffling and wiping my eyes. I needed to tell her everything, which included that I'd half-lied to the person I spoke to on the phone about the last time I saw them. "Actually, I didn't go into work today. The last time I saw them was around noon. I'm sorry...I should've been honest about that right away. I don't know why I lied. I just didn't want it to be...I don't know, I didn't want it to make me look bad."

"So you were home at noon with them?" she asked, not missing a beat, though McGuire was scribbling furiously.

"No, I..." *Just spit it out, Palmer. Gray is missing. We don't have time for this.* "I followed my husband to a woman's house this morning. A woman I believe he may be cheating on me with."

Finally, I'd gotten a reaction from her. Her eyes opened wider, lips thinning. "You...you believe your husband has been having an affair?"

I just needed to explain it all. I didn't care anymore. I just wanted Gray home and safe. "I don't know for sure. I came home early from work on Monday, and he was gone, which struck me as odd. So, I followed him the next morning, and he met with a woman at a restaurant down the street from us. I had a feeling he was going to do it again today, and so I followed him to her house. He took Gray with him there." I wasn't going to mention that I'd already followed the woman to her house. I was doing enough damage, based on the skeptical look she was giving me. "They were there until around noon and then, when he left, I did, too. But when I got home, he wasn't here."

"Why didn't you mention this before?" she asked, the warmth gone from her tone. I'd messed up. Big time.

"I wasn't intentionally leaving it out, but it's embarrassing. Right now, though, what I care about is finding

Gray. It's all I care about. Making sure he's safe. Making sure they're both safe. Please just find him," I sobbed.

"Well, the best way to do that is for you to tell us the truth. From the beginning. We can't do our jobs if we don't have all the information. Do you understand?"

I nodded, grabbing a new tissue from the coffee table and dabbing my eyes. "Of course. I'm sorry."

"Okay, so did Ben know you were suspicious about the alleged affair?"

"I don't think so. I never brought it up to him, and he never mentioned it. I was careful not to be seen when I did follow him. I was...cheated on by my ex, and he managed to lie to me every time and keep me stringing along. I wanted to see it for my own eyes rather than asking Ben and allowing him the space to lie to me. I have enough experience to know if they are caught in a lie, they'll just find new ways to hide it."

Her expression changed ever so slightly, less of a wrinkle on her forehead, less judgment in her eyes. A muscle from her jaw relaxed. She'd been cheated on before, I thought. Or knew someone who had. In this day and age, who didn't?

"Do you know the woman he met with?"

"Not personally, no. But I found her online. Her name's Katie and she's a food blogger from Crestview."

"And do you know her last name? You said you know her address?"

"I know where she lives, but I don't have an address. I can give you directions or...take you there. I don't know her last name, though. Her profile didn't have it."

"Can you show me her profile?"

I nodded, lifting my phone from the coffee table. My vision was blurry with tears, but it didn't take me long to pull her up. I turned the phone around and Kessler looked it over, passing it to McGuire, who wrote something down. She handed the phone back to me.

"Thank you. If you can give us whatever information you have on her, directions to her house, that sort of thing, that'll give us a good head start. And you said Ben doesn't have any friends? What about his family? Could he have gone to stay with them?"

"His parents are divorced, and they haven't spoken in years. There was some big falling out. Ben doesn't like to talk about it. I've never even met them."

The muscle in her jaw tightened again. "Do you know where they're located?"

"I know they live out of state, and I know their names, but I don't have much else on them." I scoffed, realizing how pathetic I must sound. "Ben never even told me which state they live in."

She looked at her partner, and I could see it all over their faces. They thought I was crazy, that Ben was leaving me, that I'd made a mistake, that I was wasting their time. I sucked in a sharp breath. "I just want my son back. Please just…please help me. Even if Ben's leaving me, I just want to see my son. I need to know he's safe."

She nodded, cocking her head to the side. "We're going to put a few calls in, okay? Check with area hospitals, check police reports, check in with this Katie, check in with his old employer, see if we can track down his parents. In the meantime, I want you to sit tight, okay? I know you'll want to help, to go out and look for them, but the best thing you can do is just be here when he gets back." *If.* "If he does, or if you hear from him, you're going to have to call me, okay? Keep in touch with me, and I'll do the same."

I nodded. "Of course. Will you…I mean, will you put out an Amber Alert for Gray? I get them on my phone sometimes for other…missing children." The words hurt to say. The thought of seeing Gray's picture on one hurt even more. *Please, no. Please be safe. Please come home.*

"One step at a time," she said, pulling out a notepad of her own for the first time. "Right now, we don't even know that they're missing, just that they haven't come home. Gray hasn't legally been kidnapped if he's with his father, even if you didn't give him permission to take him."

"But I'm his mother," I cried, panic settling further down in my stomach. "Don't I have a say in where he is? He can't just…he can't just take him, can he?"

She was solemn, refusing to answer. "We're going to focus on finding them with every resource we have, but we have no reason to believe Ben would be a threat to your son, do we?"

"Ben would never hurt Gray," I said quickly. "He loves him." *But maybe not me.* "We have to find him…"

"That's great news, Palmer. Great. That means we are just trying to find out where they ended up. Why they left. We'll start digging into his past, his bank records, everything. It's hard for people to go missing for too long these days, okay?" The warm smile was back. "I know this is scary, but I promise you we're doing everything we can to bring that baby home to you."

I felt cool tears lining my eyes as I nodded. That was all I wanted. All I cared about. I needed Gray to be safe. I needed him to be home. I needed my baby back with me. I should've followed them closer. Should've spoken up sooner. If I had, I wouldn't have lost my son. If I had, things would be so different.

CHAPTER SEVENTEEN

The next morning, I paced the house. Truth be told, I never stopped pacing. Ben never called. He never came home. Gray was still gone. Ben had taken Gray somewhere. He'd taken him away from me. But where... and why? What had I done that was so wrong?

My breasts ached from the need to pump, but I couldn't bear it. Doing so only made me think of Gray, and to do that was taking a dagger to my heart, plunging its sharp blade into my most sensitive places. Had I done enough? Had I loved him enough? Had I smiled at him, cuddled him enough? Was I enough for him? What if I never saw my son again? Were these weeks, these mere days enough to satisfy me? To give him a memory of me at all? I'd grown him in my belly, cared for him, loved him, fought for hours to bring him into the world before having my stomach torn open to pull him free. I'd done so much and would do everything over again, but would any of that matter? If something had happened to them? If Ben had run off?

Nothing would matter to me anymore.

I thought losing Nate after finding out he'd been having an affair would be the worst pain I'd ever experienced, but this, no, this was worse. This was fire to my insides and scraping of my bones. Pulling at the tender nerves on every frayed part of the shell that remained in my place. Without Gray, I was nothing. Without Gray, I'd cease to exist. I was sure of it. I'd fall to the ground, nothing left of me but ash. The charred remains of a woman who'd lost the most important thing to her. Someone would sweep me away or the breeze would carry me off, and no one would know. No one would speak of my pain or know that it existed. My pain is not the kind you talk about. It's the kind that's swept under the rug at family get-togethers, where I'd become that cousin who lost her son. That niece whose husband ran away. The girl with the missing child. And with time, that would all fade. I'd be left with nothing. I'd be nothing.

I stared around the house, its walls mostly bare, and entirely bare of pictures of my son. I had three printed photos total from the hospital, and now one of those was being passed around by the police. I hadn't even thought to ask if I'd get it back when she asked to keep it.

I had a few snapshots on my phone, as well as the blurry photos of him with Kat, but nothing more.

A knock on my door pulled me from my thoughts, and I sprang forward, hope swelling in my chest so quickly I felt like it may burst.

I swung open the door, shocked to see a familiar face.

"Dannika?" I wiped my cheeks, though the tears were

long dried. I felt my brows knit together in confusion. "What are you doing here?"

"I came to check on you," she said, stepping further into the house. "I'm worried."

I shut the door once she was inside and turned to face her. "You didn't have to come." I was so relieved to see her, though. To see any familiar face at this point.

"Well, I know you, and I know it's not like you to miss work this much. Howie's covering for you, saying you're taking meetings and whatnot, but I wanna know the truth, Palmer. Is everything okay?" She glanced behind me. "Where is everybody?"

I shook my head. "They—" My voice quivered and cracked, and I stopped, unable to prevent the tears I felt.

Concern clouded her expression. "Palmer, what is it?" She reached for me, touching my arms, and I fell into hers, letting my weight—the weight of the world—be a shared burden between the two of us. I sobbed, my body convulsing with heavy, raddled breaths. She was still for a moment before her arms made their way around me and she patted my back. "Shhh…" she soothed. "It's going to be okay, I'm sure. We'll make it okay." She whispered niceties into my ear, patting my back and nodding until my last tear had dried. I felt powerless, ashamed of my break-down. It was accomplishing nothing. I didn't have time to be sad.

When I pulled away, I looked at her, shaking my head. How could I even put into words what had happened? "Dani, they're…they're just gone."

She stared at me, one brow lifting slightly. "Who's

gone? Gone where?" She brushed a piece of hair from my eyes.

"Ben and Gray. They're missing. I don't know." My shoulders fell. "I don't know anything. Ben never came home yesterday. I can't get a hold of him. He has Gray, and they're just...gone."

Her jaw dropped, and she reached for my arms again. "Palmer...oh...oh my god, I'm so sorry. What can I do? What are *you* doing? Why didn't you tell me?"

"I'm still processing, I think. And I just keep worrying that I'll tell people, and maybe that makes it real somehow. Like, if I just keep it to myself, maybe he'll just walk through the door."

She cocked her head to the side with sympathy. "Do you really think that's going to happen? It has to, right? Where else would he be? I don't..." She trailed off, running a finger over her lips.

"I have to believe it could. Otherwise, what am I saying? They're just gone? Both of them? I can't give up on Ben. He'll do the right thing. He'll come home. He has to come home. He has to bring Gray back to me, right? He has to." I blinked back tears at the possibilities swirling through my head. He had to bring him home.

"Yes, he does. He will. I'm sure this is all just a misunderstanding. Ben loves you. We aren't giving up." Her expression was fierce as she shook her head, nudging me toward the couch. "Come on. Let's make a plan. When did they go missing, exactly? We can figure this out."

"Yesterday around noon..." I hesitated. Dannika had been there for me during my last breakup. She'd taken care of me, comforted me, encouraged me to get back out there. How would she feel if she knew that I'd managed to mess this new relationship up too? Would she start to see a pattern? Wonder if I'm worthy of any kind of love?

"Palmer, was Ben who you were talking about when you told Ty your friend's husband was having an affair?" she asked, her lips pressed together.

I sucked in a breath and held it, breaking eye contact. I knew she knew, but it didn't make it any easier. When I looked back at her, I'd given my answer.

"Son of a bitch," she said, slapping her knee. "Who is she? Do I know her?"

"She's a food blogger from Crestview. Katie something."

She wrinkled her nose. "A food blogger? Is that a real job?"

I smiled sadly. "Apparently."

"Are you okay?" She shook her head as she asked. "Of course you aren't." She paused. "And Crestview, really? She's small town? Ben always seemed so sophisticated and...you know, *worldly,* I guess," she said, shoving a shoulder forward. "He loved the city too much. I can't believe he'd be interested in anyone from Crestview."

She was trying to make me feel better, but it didn't work. What she was really saying was that Ben went against his type to cheat on me with her...that's how unhappy I made him. Just like Nate.

"So, have you checked with her? I mean, could he be with her? Do you have a way to contact her? I'll do it for you, if you want. Actually, scratch that, you are a strong, beautiful, confident woman. You should do it. You deserve the chance to confront her." She rambled more and more the angrier she got, and I loved her for it. Confrontation was not what I wanted. Truth be told, I didn't care about Kat. I just wanted Gray home and safe. It was as if someone had launched me forward, then suspended me in midair without warning. I was waiting, my breath caught, my arms and legs ready to move with no direction or inclination when they would again. I wanted to take action, but there was no action to take. I had no idea where my family was, and I couldn't imagine any worse feeling than that.

"I don't want to confront her," I said, shaking my head solemnly. "I just want to get them both home. I don't even care what he's done now, I just want to know they're okay. I need to see my son. I need to."

"I know, sweetie," she whispered, brushing a strand of hair from my eyes again and tucking it behind my ear. "I know. I do. I get it. And we will find them. We're going to figure out what's going on, okay? Do you think it's a possibility he's with her? That'd be the first place I'd look."

"I don't think so," I said, shaking my head. "I followed him to her house yesterday, but he left. I went back there later when I couldn't find him, and her husband was home."

"She has a *husband?*" She clicked her tongue. "Wow. Okay. Well...have you called the police yet? I know it seems like a big step—"

"I did," I confirmed. "They're working on it, but I don't know when I'll hear. Or if."

"Okay, so what can we do? What can *I* do?" She clasped her hands together in front of her.

"I don't know if there's anything any of us can do. The police say we should just wait to hear back."

She pursed her lips, giving me a look that clearly said *no way in hell.* "Mmkay, we're going to call that a *friendly suggestion*, and then we're going to get our asses out there and find your baby. We know Ben better than anyone. We know how he thinks, what he likes. We have to go, Palmer. Where should we start?"

My heart filled with hope, though I desperately didn't want it to be. The last thing I needed right then was hope. It made things so much more difficult. I needed anger and determination and fear. I needed to keep moving, to keep searching, to not give up. Hope was a fruitless emotion with no action behind it. Hope was waiting for something good to happen, making a birthday wish; action required so much more. I couldn't allow myself to be filled with anything that wasn't propelling me forward, finding me solutions.

"I want to talk to her, but if she's not behind this, it seems pointless."

"Well, let's go over there and just see what she has to say. Maybe, even if she doesn't know where he is, maybe she can give us a few places to look. I know it'll be hard, but we need to turn over every stone."

AN HOUR LATER, we'd pulled into Crestview. Dannika drove, and I directed, my eyes too filled with tears to be of much use behind the wheel.

"It's just on this street up ahead," I told her, pointing to the street sign and making a mental note of the name. *Blakemore.*

She turned on her blinker and pulled onto the street, slowing down as she waited for me to tell her which one we were looking for.

I couldn't.

I couldn't say anything, do anything, but stare at the house with my heartbeat thudding in my ears, my face growing hot. She glanced over at me, noticing my expression. "Is it that one?"

I nodded, barely, unable to breathe. *No. No. This isn't happening. It isn't possible.*

The lone cottage was empty, cleaned out. The windows were bare, revealing the empty rooms inside. The lawn held a red and blue FOR SALE sign.

How had the house been emptied so quickly? And why? Why was she selling it? Where had she gone? Where had her husband gone? What was happening?

She slowed to a stop in front of the house. "She was here yesterday?" Her tone said she didn't believe me, but I hoped that wasn't true. I needed her to believe me. I needed someone to.

"Yes, she was. With Ben and Gray both. The house was still full then. There were blinds and curtains. In the back, there's a tree house, and I climbed into it to watch them."

She sucked in a breath, studying the house. "Okay. Well, what did you see? Just them hanging out? Was anyone else there?"

"No, it was just the three of them. Ben and Gray left after about an hour."

"And now she's gone…" she mused. "Hm."

"Why did she leave, Dannika? What do you think it means?"

"I don't know," she said, shaking her head while keeping her eyes locked on the house. "But I'll tell you one thing, I don't believe it's a coincidence that she and Ben disappeared on the same day."

"I agree. It's too much of a coincidence, but what does it mean? Where could they have gone? Do you think they're together somehow? Or maybe she's hurt them?" My skin grew cold. "She wouldn't have hurt them, would she?"

She was silent, seemingly lost in thought. "I don't know, but I think you should tell the police about this."

"They already know where she lives. They may know she's gone, too."

"Either way, you should tell them. They should be looking into this..." She didn't finish her sentence, but she didn't need to. I could hear the end of the statement in her silence. *Before it's too late.* I wouldn't admit it to Dannika, but I'd spent much of my night researching missing persons statistics. We had seventy-two hours before our chances of ever finding them went drastically low. Less than that now. We were in the countdown and, with no evidence to help us, my husband and child had disappeared into the wind, and there was a very good chance I'd never see them again.

I sniffled, refusing to let any new tears fall as I pulled out my phone and dialed the non-emergency line again. I asked to speak to Officer Kessler once I'd been patched through, and I was placed on hold.

"Kessler."

"Hi, this is Palmer Lewis. Ben Lewis' wife."

"Yes, yes, Palmer. Hi. I was just getting ready to call you, funnily enough. Is everything all right?"

"I wanted to tell you I came back to Kat's house in Crestview, and she's moved out. It...it looks like she's selling it. It's completely empty. I know you said I shouldn't come, but I did, and I wanted you to know."

She was silent. "I see. Palmer, listen, I can send someone out to the house to check it out, maybe look up the deed to see the name of the owner. Do you have the address now?"

I recited it to her now that I knew it. "Great, thank you. Hey, while I have you... Do you know anything about several one-thousand-dollar transfers from your accounts to a separate account?"

My blood ran cold. "What?"

"It looks like there's been a transfer for one thousand dollars a month for the last six months from your account to one at a different bank."

"Six months?"

"That's what it looks like. Since you married Ben. Do you know what they were for?"

"I...I have no idea. I haven't looked at the account in a while." *Ben does that.* I didn't want to say it. When Ben took over the bills, it seemed like the most natural thing. I was pregnant. I was dealing with a lot. I was going to be the one working, so why shouldn't he be the one doing the finances? Had I really been so naïve? Had I really made this mistake again?

"Well, you should look at it and get back with me, okay? We're working on tracing where the payments ended up, but I just wanted you to be aware. You may want to contact your bank about closing the account..." She trailed off. "Also, when we were looking through your account, I noticed a charge yesterday at around two to the Stovesand Marina. Have any idea what that was about?"

I closed my eyes. The marina? We hadn't been there since we found out we were expecting Gray. I pictured the early days of our relationship, Ben taking me out in the little red rowboat from his childhood. My earliest memories of falling in love with him are filled with salty air, tanned skin, and cool water. "No. I have...no idea. He did rent a slip there for a while, for his boat. But we haven't been there since before Gray was born. Does that mean he was there?"

"It could've been an online purchase. We're working on figuring it out. So, is Ben a big water guy? Does he sail? Does he still keep his boat there?"

"He likes to boat, sure. I mean, he had a rowboat from his childhood. It was...it was tiny. He sold it when we found out about Gray because he couldn't justify the cost. We'd never have taken Gray on it. Could we have found his trail?"

"We're still looking into everything. One more question."

"Okay..."

"We contacted your property manager about getting video surveillance from your apartment building. He mentioned that you guys just had an attempted break-in. When I looked you up, it looks like he was right. Two days before Ben disappeared. Is there a reason you didn't mention it?"

I swallowed. "I'd forgotten, to be honest. Things have just been so crazy...it was the last thing on my mind."

"Information like this could be very important to your case. We need to make sure you aren't omitting details like these."

"Do you think they're related? The break-in and their disappearance? Do you really think someone could've taken them?"

She was quick to reply. "I don't want you to panic. We'll know more when we get the surveillance footage from your landlord today."

"Surveillance footage? But...there won't be any. Ben said the cameras here don't work."

I could hear her typing something, but she stopped at my last remark. "I'm sorry, what?"

"Ben said after the break-in that he contacted our super and he said the cameras don't work. That's why the police couldn't get the footage after the break-in."

"Palmer..." She hesitated. "Ben never contacted your super. I just spoke with him myself. We have the footage from the day of the attempted break-in, and no one entered the building or left during the time Ben said the attempt happened. There was no one suspicious around the building that day at all. The report says our officers called and relayed that information to Ben. He didn't tell you any of this?"

I touched my fingers to my chin, my voice breathless. "No..."

"Hm. Well, we're getting the footage within the hour, so we should know soon when or if Ben came home yesterday after you saw him last. I just wanted to ask you some questions in case there was an obvious explanation to some of the things that seem to be bugging me. I'll be in touch as we learn more, okay?"

I nodded, though she couldn't see me, and I felt Dannika's gaze burning into me. She squeezed my arm from the side, giving me gentle encouragement.

"Of course. Th-thank you."

As I ended the call, I looked over at Dannika, who seemed to sense the concern. "What did she say?"

I blinked rapidly, staring off into the distance as I processed all I'd learned. "They think Ben used our card at the marina yesterday...and...there's money missing from our accounts. A lot of money. He lied to me about someone trying to break in. He said he checked with our super, said there was no footage... He lied about so much, Dannika."

Dannika's jaw tightened. "So what do they think? Was he planning to disappear all along?"

She didn't say and, until that moment, it hadn't occurred to me. If Ben was planning to disappear, why would he take Gray, too? What was he planning to do?

Sickness washed over me, and I shoved the door of the car open, spewing vomit onto the pavement. How could I have trusted him?

CHAPTER EIGHTEEN

B ack at the house, I scrolled through my online banking from my laptop, looking over the transactions I'd missed over and over again. One thousand dollars, once a month. I'd never noticed. As quickly as money came into the account, Ben had drained it. The savings I'd been so worried about halving with him was running lower than I'd imagined. I thought he'd been putting money into it each month, but from the looks of it, the only money he was moving was going out.

I'd moved past self-deprecating. No longer was I blaming myself, but instead, I was filled with fury for what he'd done. How he'd tricked me. What he'd let me believe.

Dannika had hesitantly left to eat dinner with Ty and the kids, trying to convince me to come along, but I couldn't do it. I didn't know how to function when my child was missing. I didn't know what I was allowed to think, what I was allowed to feel. I couldn't help being numb to it all. It was the safest option. Happiness was far away, like a distant memory. Anger was predominant.

I opened up Kat's Instagram, searching through her recent posts. To my surprise, she hadn't posted anything new since the day she rated the cheesecake. I searched through her posts. It was rare there weren't at least two posts a day, but now she'd gone several days without any new content. It was as if she'd fallen off the face of the planet, much like my husband. Much like my son.

Where are you, Ben?

I clicked to view her website, where she'd posted a few of her favorite restaurants and a handful of her reviews. It wasn't as active as her Instagram, but each post contained several comments from happy fans. She'd done well building a brand for herself. I was incredibly tempted to comment on something—to demand that she come forward and tell me what she knew, but I stopped. I couldn't lash out. I wanted things to be amicable. I wanted my child to come home. I had to play their game, no matter the cost.

My phone began buzzing from across the room where it was charging, and I leapt up. The storm was brewing outside, the sky dark and thunder rumbling. Normally, I loved storms. Since the day of their disappearance, the weather made me feel more isolated than ever.

When I saw the number on the screen, my stomach went tense.

"Hello?"

"Palmer? It's Officer Kessler." She paused. "Listen, I have some news, and I wanted to be sure you heard it before the news stations start picking it up."

My throat was suddenly dry, chest tight. I couldn't quite catch my breath. "Okay…"

"Can you meet me at the marina?"

"Please tell me what it is," I begged, my heart thudding in my chest. "Please. I can't make the drive down without knowing." I placed my fingers over my lips, their trembling enough to make me mad.

"I…they found a boat, Palmer. A boat washed ashore a few hours ago. We think it was Ben's."

CHAPTER NINETEEN

The air was salty and humid, the sand dark and wet as I walked across the shore of our beach, heading to the police tent that had been set up in front of a mid-sized white boat. Police swarmed the boat, some with cameras, some with notepads, some with bags containing who knew what.

I spied Kessler right away, with Dannika just feet behind me, and headed toward her. She was talking to another officer, a short male, but when she caught my eye, they broke apart, her patting his arm before walking to meet me in the middle.

"Mrs. Lewis, thank you for meeting me." As she said my name, I noticed something different about her. A coldness. A separation. She was all business now, and that terrified me. I knew what bad news looked like before it was delivered. Between work and Nate, I'd been on the receiving end of it too many times to count.

"What's happening?" I asked, my hands shaking as I

glanced over at the boat again. It wasn't damaged or broken, from what I could tell. It looked to be in fine shape.

She followed my gaze, then brought me back to her. "The boat was found by our department this morning. Some tourists called the police and claimed that it had washed ashore, but there was no one aboard. The marina owner reported that he'd had a boat stolen last night, one that had been rented by Ben but was never returned. We've just confirmed this is that boat."

A cold chill ran over me as I heard her words in slow motion. "And...and you're sure it's my Ben?"

"We're sure. The money came from your joint account. They have a copy of his ID and CCTV footage from the time that he came to pick it up. It was just before the storm. The marina owner claims he told Ben that he should hold off on going out until the storm passed, but has no way of knowing if he did."

I sucked in a slow, steady breath. "Okay...okay. So, what does that mean? I mean, the boat's not damaged. Maybe they didn't end up taking it out after all. Maybe it broke loose."

Her eyes were sorrowful as they danced between mine. "There's quite a bit of water on the inside. It could be from the rain, but we're...we think it's likely there may have been a wave that knocked them overboard. An inexperienced sailor in a storm like that... The odds of them surviving aren't good. We can't be sure just yet, but I want you to be prepared. We've got a team headed out to search for the bodies."

The tears I'd barely been keeping at bay pushed through at that moment, and my knees collapsed underneath me, slamming me onto the wet sand. I felt the water seeping through my pants, but I couldn't care. I couldn't *breathe.* I sucked in a breath, pushing it out with force, but it was as if the air contained no oxygen. I clutched a hand to my chest. *In, out. In, out.* Whatever pain I'd experienced in my life, it was nothing compared to this. My stomach tightened the longer I thought about it, and I couldn't prevent myself from thinking about it.

I felt a hand on my back and I knew it was Dannika, but my vision and hearing were tunneling, the world around me growing faint as I fought harder to focus. My heart pounded in my chest, and I focused on it. The steady *thud thud, thud thud, thud thud.* I patted my hand to my chest, following the pattern. I had to breathe. I needed to hear the rest.

Dannika bent down next to me, an arm around my shoulders, and rested her head against mine. She didn't say a word, didn't have to, but helped shoulder my grief with her actions. "Can you tell us what will happen next?" she asked the officer.

"From all that you've told me, Palmer, I know it's hard to hear, but I believe Ben was planning to leave you. It seems like he took the money with the intent of running away when the timing was right. We believe we've located his parents, but we haven't been able to make contact. I have officers headed to their residence now to see if we can get them to confirm my suspicions. If Ben contacted them, it's likely they knew his plan. Right now, we're searching the boat to see if there's any indication of what happened, and we've got crews out searching for the..." She hesitated. "For their bodies, like I said. I believe it's just a matter of time."

I let out a sob, my fingers going to my lips.

"I'm so sorry, Palmer," Dannika whispered, squeezing me tighter.

"Does she have someone she can stay with?" Kessler asked, her voice cool and official.

"She can stay with me," Dannika said. "For as long as she needs."

I looked up at the officer, who nodded with a tight jaw. I fought back still-tunneling vision, feeling sure I was going to throw up at any moment. I couldn't breathe, couldn't feel, couldn't think. It all hurt. It hurt to cry, to inhale, to exhale, to scream. I fell further into the sand, resting on my elbows as I sobbed into the wet sand.

It wasn't possible. It wasn't.

I'd fought so hard to bring my baby into the world.

I'd grown his little lips, formed his little fingers, and someone had ripped him away from me. Everything in my future had been ripped away in the blink of an eye. No first steps, no first words, no preschool, no teaching him to swim, no watching him see the ocean for the first time. It was all just...gone. He was gone. I'd never hold my son again. Never look into his sparkling blue eyes. Never hear what his laugh would've sounded like. Never hear him call me 'Mommy.'

I couldn't catch my breath as I tried to, still face down in the sand. I didn't care enough to lift up. Dannika's hands were on my back again, pulling me up, and I heard Kessler say something.

The words were fuzzy, like my vision, and before I could focus, darkness found me.

CHAPTER TWENTY

When I awoke, I was in a room I didn't recognize at first. I looked around at the green walls and white curtains, the photos that weren't mine. It all felt like a dream.

Then the pain hit me. Slammed into me with the weight of a brick wall. It took my breath away.

My son was probably dead.

My husband was probably dead.

My husband was definitely a liar.

I still knew nothing of the truth.

I sat up, squeezing my eyes shut as the tears welled in them, blurring my vision. I grabbed the comforter, holding it to my face as I sobbed into it.

None of it felt real.

It was a nightmare I couldn't escape from.

A horror story that used me as the heroine.

Had Gray felt it? Had he cried out for me? Had it been peaceful? Painful? Had he wondered where I was? Why I couldn't save him?

Why, Ben?

I laid in bed, sobbing for what seemed like hours, my body physically incapable of moving too much. If I laid still enough, perhaps I would wake up and realize it was all a dream.

After a while, I sat up, my chest and muscles sore from the constant crying. My face was red and raw from the tears, my throat scratchy. I needed to bathe. I needed to brush my teeth. I needed to pump my milk. Still, I couldn't. I couldn't find the strength to do anything.

I lifted my phone from the nightstand and checked it. My mom had texted, checking in. She'd either seen it on the news or Dannika had filled her in. Her words were misspelled, and I knew she'd typed it while crying, too. I couldn't talk to her right then. It would only make me cry harder.

My bladder burned for relief and, eventually, I forced myself to get up rather than pee the bed in Dannika's guest bedroom. If I'd been at home, I may have chosen differently. I walked toward the bathroom and stepped into the bright light, glancing at myself in the mirror. It was as if a light had been switched off inside of me. Though it had only been hours since I'd found out what happened, it looked like years of life had been drained from my body. My skin was sallow and dull, my eyes dark. My hair stuck up in every direction, my clothes drenched in sweat and stiff from the saltwater and sand. My arms and the back of my neck had a red, itchy rash that I realized must've come from not showering when we got home. The bed was full of sand, and thanks to the salt, my skin was drier than usual. It was a bad combination, but despite the itch, I just didn't care. It was as if the caring part of me had drifted off to sea with my child. I was empty, a vessel with a beating heart and working bodily functions, but not much else.

After I'd used the restroom and washed my hands, I scooped a bit of water into my mouth to ease my dry throat, just enough to coat my tongue, and then walked from the room. I was tempted to climb back into bed, to never move again, but I needed to see if there had been any updates. I knew by now the news would be covering the story.

When I walked out of the bedroom, Dannika was sitting on the edge of the couch, folding a load of laundry. She perked up when she saw me, watching my expression. "Hey…" she said cautiously. "How are you?"

I shook my head, my voice catching in my throat before I could say anything. I felt *empty*, I supposed, was the best way to describe it. So much emptiness. "Have they…found anything?" Any*one.*

She shook her head, almost eagerly. "No, nothing."

I looked around. "Where're the kids?" I wasn't used to being in Dannika's house without it being loud, noisy, and messy. It was like some alternate reality.

Her expression changed, and I realized in an instant why they weren't there. Because from here on out, I would be the woman people felt strange for having their kids around. Like they were bragging simply by existing. Like I would wish all kids would die because mine had. "I had Ty drop them off at his mom's on his way to the office. She gets bored, and I figured you could use some quiet."

I glanced at the clock. "Shouldn't you be at work, too?" *Not me. I'm not sure I'll ever go back again.*

"I took the rest of the week off, and so did you. I called Cumberland last night after we got home. We're fine. It's being handled. I think Howie may come by later to check on you, if that's okay."

I didn't want to see anyone, but I didn't say so. Instead, I wandered into the kitchen and opened the cabinet where she kept her glasses. I pulled out a purple plastic one and filled it with tap water. As I lifted the glass to my lips, seeing the water rising toward me, I had a flash of water filling Gray's toothless mouth, filling his lungs. I coughed, spluttering up water and spewing it across the room as new tears filled my eyes. How was I supposed to go on like this? How was I going to survive it? I wasn't sure I would.

Dannika shot up the instant I coughed, rushing toward me with a towel. Without me explaining what happened, she seemed to understand. That was Dannika; she always understood. She grabbed a towel from the drawer and cleaned up my mess, watching me stand there frozen in place with the cup in my hand. I wasn't sure I'd ever be able to drink again. Maybe I wouldn't have to worry about living much longer after all. How long could a person live without water? *The rule of threes.* Three minutes without oxygen, three days without water, three weeks without food. The old saying came to my head immediately. Three days didn't seem so bad.

"Thank you," I squeaked once she'd cleaned it up. She shook her head, reaching her arms out for me. If I gave in to her hug, I was going to lose it.

She stepped forward, and I fell, crashing my weight into her chest, which she bared gracefully. Her arms engulfed me, her cheek pressed to mine, and when we pulled away, there were tears in her own eyes, an ocean of sorrow looking back at me. She kissed my forehead, pressing hers to mine. "I'm so sorry, Palmer. I don't even know what to say except I'm *so* sorry."

What could she say? There was nothing. No combination of the right words or syllables could ease the ache in my heart. It had lodged itself there permanently, a lump of bitter pain where feelings were supposed to be.

I nodded, hugging her back and letting the sobs come freely. I sniffled and snotted and cried until my body ached, and Dannika held me the whole time. I'd never been so grateful for her, even if it was a dull, muted, colorless kind of grateful. My life without Gray was, for lack of a better word, gray, and that was the cruelest amount of irony life had ever bestowed upon me.

When we broke apart, she put the cup on the counter behind us, moving it from the island, and led me into the living room to sit down on the couch.

"Do I...I mean, am I supposed to be planning a funeral for them?" My lips quivered at the question.

"I don't want you to worry about that right now. The police are still searching. Right now, we...we just wait and we...and we pray. And we trust that God is going to bring that baby back to you. If we don't have hope, Palmer, we don't have anything. You know that."

"Why would they let him take a boat out in the storm? Why wouldn't they have made him wait to get the keys if they knew the storm was coming?" I asked, my voice an octave higher. I didn't want to wait or to pray. I wanted my son back. I wanted answers. Rage felt safer than anything, so it was the one emotion I let in at its full, colorful glory. "Shouldn't there be a...a law on it or something?"

"I've been looking at the website. Apparently if they're caught in a storm, they have the ability to wait it out or bring it back for a refund. If he was already on the water by the time the storm came, maybe he thought it was safe enough to wait it out..." She trailed off, realizing she wasn't helping.

I didn't need facts. I didn't need anything besides Gray, and I knew the chances of me having him ever again were slim to none. Office Kessler had all but said so. They were looking for bodies, not survivors.

"I know we hadn't been together that long, but...I really did love Ben," I said, feeling pathetic. I grabbed a tissue as she handed me the box, scooting back on the couch and settling in next to me.

"I know you did, babe. I know."

"I thought he loved me."

"I thought he did, too. He fooled us all."

"I didn't want him to die." It's a thought that'd been in my head for a while now. No matter how angry I was with Ben, I didn't want him to die. I just wanted him to love me. To choose me. I didn't want to be an option. I wanted his proposal, his 'I do,' to have meant the same as my 'yes' and 'I do, too.' I was in love with Ben. I loved him with everything I had, and I was prepared to stay with him for the rest of our lives. Until Kat. As far as I was concerned, she ruined everything.

I knew from my experience with Nate, blaming the woman wasn't the right direction. He'd been the cheater. He'd been the liar. As far as I knew, Kat was just as much a victim in this as I was. But I had no sympathy for her, not after I watched her with Gray. Not after what she'd done.

"Of course you didn't want him to die," Dannika said, tilting her head toward her shoulder. "Of course not, Palmer. I know that. I know how much you loved him, what you sacrificed for him. If he couldn't see that, he was the one who made the mistake. No one in this world is better than you. He's blind if he couldn't see that." She squeezed my hand and paused. "I looked at the girl's profile this morning, and she's not all that great, honestly. No match for you. He was blind, and that's his fault. You can be sad that he's gone and hurt that he betrayed you. It's not either/or. You're allowed to grieve in your own way. No one can tell you how to feel right now."

"I wish they could, honestly. I don't know how to feel. Hurt, obviously. Sad. But…I just feel empty mostly. I feel like there's a huge hole inside of me where they're supposed to be. How can this be happening?"

She frowned sympathetically. "I don't know…I just don't."

"I know it's not her fault, but I want to blame her, you know? I need to be angry at someone, and I can't bring myself to feel that anger for Ben. As much as I want to."

"Be angry at her all you want." She shifted her weight on the couch, handing me a new tissue as I felt new tears forming. "That's your right. You get angry. Be furious. Be mad at her. Mad at him. Mad at the universe. And then when you're done being mad, we'll be sad and we'll cry, and then we can switch back to mad. However you're feeling, you do it, and I'll be right there with you. You can stay with Ty and me for as long as you like. We've already discussed it. Consider it an open invitation. And, if you want to move out of the apartment, we'll deal with that, too."

I hadn't even thought about the apartment, and I wasn't sure when I could. "I can't be a burden to you guys," I said, dabbing my nose.

"You, my friend, are never a burden. *You* were the only thing that got me through Momma dying during college, and this is me returning the favor in the best way I know how."

My phone chimed, and I glanced down, my eyes widening at the screen. "She made a new post..." I should've turned my notifications off for her posts, but I hadn't thought about it. She'd been silent for days now.

"Who?" Dannika asked.

I opened the app and waited for it to load. When it did, I studied it. It was a close-up picture of her sitting on the edge of a hotel bed, her hair had all been flipped to one side of her head in a casual way, her face solemn. The blue tank top she wore hung off one shoulder loosely. Despite the messy look, it was obvious her makeup had been done, albeit natural-looking. The picture was meant to look bad in a very good way.

I scrolled to read the caption.

Hey, food lovers! I'm sorry I haven't been as active lately. I've had a few things going on to disrupt my schedule (and my life honestly) and I'm working toward a new normal. Please bear with me while I

make some adjustments. **So many of you have reached out to be sure all is well, and I assure you it is. Soon, I'll be able to share all the exciting details with you, but for now, I'm sending you my love. Drop your favorite food emoji below to let me know you've seen this. Eat well, my loves. Dessert first!**

I read through it twice. What was she talking about? What changes? What things? What adjustments? What exciting news? This didn't seem like the post of a woman who'd just learned her boyfriend was missing and potentially lost at sea. Had she heard the news? If not, wasn't she worried about him?

I studied the picture, looking for a hint of emotion other than happiness in her eyes, but it wasn't there. Whatever she had with Ben, if she'd heard the news, it couldn't have been serious.

As my eyes trailed the corners of the photo, I froze, the hairs on my arms standing up as my body went cold. "Dani…"

"What is it?" she asked, her voice hesitant.

I swallowed, my throat dry again as I looked up at her and held out the phone. The words I said next sent chills down my spine as we both stared at the tiny, blue and white blanket in her background. She'd missed cropping it out by just a bit, but I'd know it anywhere. It was custom and, if I flipped it over, his name would be sewn on the bottom left hand corner. "She has Gray."

CHAPTER TWENTY-ONE

Dannika searched the picture, looking for any other clue as to where she might be, while I called Officer Kessler to let her know what we'd discovered. She swore to look into it and ended the call quickly, a new urgency in her voice, and for the first time, I realized she might truly believe me. For the first time, I was allowing myself to hope. Gray was alive, and we were going to find him.

When we'd given up on the picture, I moved back to my online banking, searching through the transactions the police still hadn't given me any updates for.

I dialed my bank, trying to get to the bottom of it once and for all.

"Midwest State Bank, this is Deb, how may I help you?"

"Deb, hi. My name is Palmer Lewis. I have a few accounts with you, and it looks like I have a transaction per month for the last several months that I don't recognize."

"Okay," she said, her tone professional and sharp. "Let's take a look. Do you have your account number?"

I recited it to her from memory and listened as she typed it in. "Can you verify the last four of your social and your birth date?"

I did as she asked and waited.

"Okay, now, which transactions are we talking about?" I heard her typing again.

"There is one a month for a thousand even and, from what I can see, it goes back six months."

She was quiet for a moment, then clicked her tongue. "I see what you mean. It looks like…yes, they're being sent out of your account to another bank via your online banking."

"Is there a way to see who the account belongs to?"

"Hmm…did you not authorize the transfers?"

"I didn't, no. I'm not sure what they are for."

"They would've had to be done with your credentials…" She trailed off. "I can't see any information on it—it looks like they were done through our third party, person-to-person pay service—but I can put in a request to be able to get more information from our back office. It may take a day or two. If you didn't do it, we can do a dispute for you, but you'd lose access to your online banking, and there's no guarantee we could get your money back. It would have to go through an investigation, especially since it isn't connected to your card. Visa disputes are a bit easier."

"Okay, that would be fine. I totally understand." I scrolled back down, noticing something else I didn't recognize. "Can you look at one other thing for me?"

"Of course," she said, noticeably less enthused to help me than before.

"On September ninth, there's a charge for one hundred nineteen dollars to a store called FunnyFuzzy. Can you tell me what that is?"

I heard her typing. "One nineteen...there it is. Okay, that was on your card, but you're past the point of disputing it. You only have six months."

"I don't need to dispute it. I just want to know what it was," I snapped, growing irritated with her attitude.

I heard her click. "There's a website and a phone number here. Do you want both?"

"Yes, please." She recited them, and I pointed at the pen in front of Dannika, holding out my hand. She passed it to me, and I jotted the information down on a scrap of paper. "Thank you so much. Listen, is there a way to close the card that the charge came from? I think it's possible we've been hacked."

"That's definitely possible. Do you want to lock it or just close it?"

"Close it, please. And thank you."

"You're welcome. I'll close it out here in just a moment and I'll get this request put in for more information on the transfers, too. Once we have that, someone'll give you a call. Is this still a good phone number for you?" she asked, reading it off.

"Yes, that's perfect. Thank you again."

I ended the call and looked at Dannika. "They aren't sure who the transfers were for, but I also noticed this for a store I've never heard of." I pulled the laptop closer toward me and typed in the website the teller had given me. It loaded within seconds, and I furrowed my brow. *What?* It was a gag gift site, loaded with fake dog poo, zen garden litter boxes, giant rolls of toilet paper, fake pregnancy tests, fake bed bugs, whoopie cushions, vulgar coffee mugs, and more.

"Maybe he was getting something for someone at work?" she asked, shrugging one shoulder and looking as appalled as I felt.

"Yeah, maybe…" The site was atrocious, and anyone who could find most of it funny terrified me. I closed the laptop and hung my head back against the sofa. Dead end after dead end. Where were we supposed to look next? What options could I still dig into?

My phone rang again, and I glanced down, surprised to see the bank's number on my screen. Dannika's eyes were wide and fearful as she watched me answer.

"Hello?"

"Ms. Lewis? This is Deb from the bank."

"Oh, hey."

"Hey, I know you asked me to close out the card ending in five, seven, three, three, but we just had a charge attempt to go through. I wanted to verify with you that you wanted me to refuse it?"

My heart pounded, my nerves on high alert, as I sat up straighter. "What charge?" I asked, my breathing loud in my own ears. Dannika moved closer, and I met her eyes, hope in mine.

"It was for a flight. Six hundred seventy-nine dollars."

I stood from the couch, the room spinning as I learned the new information. My entire body began to tremble as I paced. "Let it go through."

"Are you sure? If I do—"

"I won't dispute it, Deb, don't worry. Just let it go through. Can you tell me which airline it is?"

"It's Coastal Carolina."

"To where?"

"I can't see that information, ma'am." Dammit. I slapped a hand against my temple.

"Okay, fine, let it go through." This was my chance—my only chance to find them.

"Okay, I have. It's approved."

I hung up the phone without a goodbye and darted back to the laptop. "They're going to try to get away."

"Who?" Dannika asked.

"Whoever's using Ben's card. Ben, Kat, I don't know."

"How do you know?"

"They just used his card to book a flight."

"Stop them!" Dannika shouted, pointing out the door.

"I couldn't," I told her, typing in the airport to find the phone number. "This is my only chance to track them down. If I know where they'll be, I can catch them. I can get him back, Dani." She didn't look convinced. "I know it's a risk, but I have to do it."

"I think you should let the police handle it, Palmer. What are you going to do? Attack them? Rip Gray from her arms?"

"Whatever it takes," I told her, and I believe we both knew I meant it. I would've burned the place down if it meant saving my son. I dialed the airline. When I was connected with a representative, I asked, "Hi, I just booked a flight with you, and I didn't get a receipt in my email. If I have my card number, can you pull it up and make sure the payment went through?"

"I'd be happy to. What's that card number?"

I opened the online banking tab again and found Ben's card, reading it off to her.

"Thank you," she said, typing it in. "Yes, it does look like it went through."

"And what flight am I on? I'm just making sure I did it right."

"Looks like you're scheduled to leave this afternoon at three forty-five headed to Los Angeles."

My body went numb. "And...can you tell me how many tickets I purchased? There should've been three."

I heard her click something. "Yes, looks like two adults and one child who will be riding on a lap."

I tried to swallow, but my throat was too dry. It was true. They were taking my child across the country. If I didn't catch them today, I might lose him forever.

"Thank you so much," I said, my voice powerless as I hung up.

"What did she say?" Dannika asked, eyeing me with worry.

"They're flying to Los Angeles this afternoon."

She stood, jerking my arm up so I would join her. "We have to go. We'll call the police on the way. We can't let them get on the flight."

I was already in action, running toward the bedroom.

I was going to get him back. I had to. There was no other option. I'd sooner die than lose my child again.

CHAPTER TWENTY-TWO

The airport was packed. We were surrounded by frazzled travelers, irritated businessmen, and exhausted families, all in a hurry, some rather lost. We stood in the center of the open terminal, watching as the room began to fill. Outside, the police were waiting. At the first sign of Ben, Kat, or Gray, they were going to jump out of their unmarked cars and stop them. We were the last line of defense. The ones going to stop them if they somehow made it past the police outside. To my far right, another plainclothes officer stood, just in case things got out of hand, but Officer Kessler assured me she didn't think that would be the case. I wasn't sure if she was lying or if she just wanted to keep me calm.

Truth be told, they didn't want us there in the first place. They wanted to handle it. But they would've had to arrest me to keep me away. They knew who they were looking for based on pictures, but I *knew* them. I knew the tiny idiosyncrasies of Ben's face and the way he moved. I knew the way Gray smelled. I knew the evil in Kat's eyes.

I knew them better than any of the officers, and if there was any chance they were going to sneak past and get on the plane, I couldn't let that happen. If I lost Gray again today, I was sure I wouldn't survive it.

I spun around in circles, my eyes searching and watching the doors, the windows, traveling up to the high ceiling then back down. He had to be there.

Every time someone with strawberry-blonde hair entered, my stomach lurched, only to be let down. The flight was boarding now, the first call for it, and still I hadn't seen them. A few people had come in carrying babies, but Gray wasn't one of them.

I looked at Dannika across the crowded room, her expression painfully hopeful. I knew she saw the weight in my eyes. She knew what this meant. She knew I might not survive not finding him. She was holding me up by a thread, though she looked to be barely holding on herself.

The officer in the corner looked serious. His eyes scanned the crowd with intense precision. He checked every face, examined every piece of luggage. He was doing his job, emotionless, and I knew it was what was needed. I couldn't keep myself in check; it was what they'd said when they warned me to stay away. I'd sworn I could. I'd argued. Fought. And as long as I felt filled with such intense, palpable hope, I'd been able to do it. Now, though, as time was winding down, the air was deflating from my chest, and we still hadn't found them. I found myself beginning to lose it again. Every second that passed, I felt an ounce of hope dissipating. I'd been so close to him, I could practically feel him in my arms again, but I'd been wrong. I could tell it by the look on the officer's face. By the look on Dani's. By the sinking feeling in my gut.

When the final boarding call came and I spied Kessler walking inside, I knew. The lump in my throat was so big, I couldn't swallow. My chest was tight as I watched her approach me, an apology in her eyes.

She shook her head slightly as she grew nearer. "I'm sorry, Palmer."

"No," I argued. "He has to be here. He has to. Someone booked the flight with Ben's card... Why would they do that?"

She hesitated, watching as the officer from the far side of the room grew closer. "We don't know. It's...well, it's possible it was a diversion."

"You think they *wanted* me to see the charge?"

She nodded stiffly. "I think it's likely."

"But why? Why would they do that?"

"Wanting to distract us would be the most obvious reason. But we can try to get a subpoena to get the airline to release the IP address where the purchase was made. If we can get that—"

"We don't have that kind of time," I cried. "What if they're getting on a plane right now? What if they're taking my son?"

"I know this is scary," Kessler said. "I do. I promise you we're doing everything in our power. We're working on getting the flight manifest to see if they got on the plane, but it's *very* unlikely they did. If they managed to, we'll have officers waiting in LA to pick them up when they land."

"So, what do we do now?"

"You go home. Let us do our jobs, Palmer. I appreciate all the help you've given, and it's possible you've set us on the right track, but all the time we're spending talking is time I can't spend looking for your son. Okay? It's hard enough because he was believed to be on the boat with your husband, and right now I'm having a hard time convincing anyone he wasn't. I'm trusting your gut as a mother, but there's little else I can do if you don't, at some point, let me do my job."

I nodded, fighting back tears of rage. I knew she was right, somewhere deep, deep down, but the truth was none of them cared about Gray as much as I did. None of them were as emotionally invested as I was. None of them were sure they would quit breathing if this case went cold.

"I'm sorry," she said again, her tone softer. "I promise I'll call you the second we have any news."

"Thank y—" A sob interrupted my words, and I forced myself to walk away, away from the place where my hope died once again, away from the officer whose eyes said she believed this was a lost cause.

All around me, people bustled, in a hurry to start their vacation or make it to a wedding. Their next chapters were starting, but I had the strangest sensation my last chapter was ending.

CHAPTER TWENTY-THREE

That evening, the movie was droning on in the background, while Ty, Dannika, and I sat on the couch in pure silence. My mind raced a mile a minute as I tried to come up with something new to do, something new to search. There had to be something. I couldn't give up. I refused to.

"Maybe we should go back by the girl's house," Dannika offered, and I was relieved to see I wasn't the only one plagued by endless worry.

"Do you think we'd find anything different?" I asked.

"What if we talked to the realtor? Maybe we could ask what happened to the current owners?"

Ty looked like he wanted to say something, his mouth twisted in thought, but he kept quiet.

"Do you think it could work?" I asked.

"Realtors are talkers. They want you to feel at ease. It's worth a shot," Dannika said.

"I don't think she'd tell you specifics. Or that this girl

would've told her realtor specifics if she was really trying to be hidden," Ty pointed out, slowing down his speech when he caught a glimpse of the scowl on Dannika's face. He added quickly, "But we can't totally rule it out."

Dannika picked up her phone from the arm of the couch and looked at me. "What was the address again? We'll call."

I told her, the address now burned into my memory. The last place I saw my son alive. The last place I may ever.

She typed it in, and I watched her thumb scroll across her lighted screen. "I'm not finding the realtor listing. Do you remember the name of the company?"

I shook my head, another wave of defeat washing over me. "It was blue and red..." A sigh escaped me, and I rested my elbows on my knees, chin in my palms. How could I have not thought to remember something so potentially important?

"It's okay," she said. She stood, grabbing her keys from the basket on the shelf over the fireplace. "Let's go."

"Wait, we're—okay," Ty said, not bothering to argue. I jumped into action, and he followed suit, flipping off the television and light as the three of us raced out the front door without a second's hesitation.

The drive to Crestview was a bit shorter than normal, as Dannika lived on that side of Oceanside, but we drove it in complete silence. Everything around me seemed to be silent lately. People just didn't know what to say. The police, Howie, my parents, Ty and Dannika. Everything had fallen by the wayside. Who cared about menial, everyday things when your family was missing? How could I carry on a conversation about a movie or laundry or dinner when my child was with a stranger?

Somehow, Dannika and Ty's silence carried less weight than anyone else's.

We pulled up in front of the house, which looked much the same as the last time, its blinds open, rooms empty. The sign had blown over in the yard, but I read the name off and typed it in.

I left her a voicemail and Ty made a lap around town as we waited for a callback. In the town square, I noticed one sole business open: Sassy Snips.

"Hey, can you stop for a second?" I asked, and Ty immediately slowed, pulling into a parking space across from the store. I pushed my door open from the back seat. "I'll be right back, okay?"

They nodded, looking confused, but I didn't look back as I crossed the street and hurried into the shop. Toshia was washing out a bowl of dye in the back corner of the empty store while Carolyn swept up.

"Can we help you?" Carolyn asked, squinting her eyes. She was trying to decide how she knew me, but recognition flooded Toshia's eyes.

"Did you decide to come back for those highlights?" she asked, an uneasy smile on her face.

"I'm sorry, no. I just...I had something come up, and I had to leave in a hurry. I was actually here to see what you could tell me about the client you were helping while I waited. Kat."

"Kat?" she asked. "Why?"

Carolyn stopped sweeping as I walked past, watching the interaction curiously. Toshia shut off the water and smacked her hands against the side of the sink before drying them off.

"You said she lives around here, right? Does she come in often?"

"Why are you asking?" she pressed.

I knew I couldn't tell her the truth. She would protect Kat at all costs. So, I lied. "I legally can't tell you, but it's really important that I find her. I believe she may be in danger." It surprised me how easily the lie came.

Toshia's jaw dropped. "Oh my god."

"Do you know how I can get a hold of her?"

She shook her head. "I really don't. She just moved out of her parents' rental place yesterday. Her husband's job ended, and they moved back home."

"Back? Back where? I thought she lived here?" She looked over my shoulder, where I knew Carolyn must be standing. "It's really important, Toshia."

"They have a house in Red River. I honestly don't know the address. She grew up here in Crestview, but when she got married, they moved away. Her husband's latest job took him away for a year, so she moved back home and rented her childhood home from her parents. It was the first I'd seen of her in years."

"Okay." I sucked in a breath, thinking quickly. "And you said her name's Katie, right? Do you know her last name?"

"Katherine, technically. But Katie or Kat, yes. Her last name was Thompson before she got married... I'm not sure if she ever changed it. I'm sorry, I really don't know much else. Have you checked her blog? Her mom says she's always on it."

"I have. She hasn't posted much lately."

"With her husband home, the new baby, and the move, that makes sense. I can give you her parents' address, but they're probably in Red River—"

My breathing caught at her words, my fingers clenching into a fist. "Wait. What do you mean? What new baby?"

She nodded. "They just adopted a baby. They'd had a really hard time having one... I didn't know they were adopting, but it was perfect timing, really, with his job ending."

I swallowed, my vision beginning to blur. "You said her parents are gone, too?"

"Oh, I don't know that for sure. Kat's been telling everyone they were getting ready to adopt a baby. The paperwork was all finalized; they were just waiting on the placement, which she said would be any day. When I drove by Friday afternoon, it looked like they were over there packing up her stuff. So, I'd say they finally got the little one, and now that her husband's home, they'll be moving back to Red River. If I know her parents, I'd say they took them up to Red River to help them settle in. I don't know when they'll be back. They just live around the corner, the house next door to Kat's. Do you want the address?"

I shook my head, running from the store without another word. They had Gray, and they were claiming him as their own.

What had happened to Ben?

Who were these people?

And, most importantly, what did they want with my son?

CHAPTER TWENTY-FOUR

"I think we should call the police," Ty said, his voice firm, once I'd told them what I'd learned. I was practically in hysterics, and Dannika seemed torn between my panic and Ty's calm.

"I mean, I agree, but I don't want to just go home and wait. There has to be something else we can do."

"What more can you do, Palmer? The rest should be up to the police," he said.

"The police move at a snail's pace. You know that better than anyone. We've seen that just over the course of this investigation. Everything helpful up to this point has been found by me. If I wait and let them work through the red tape, it may be too late. We have to go there. We have to find him."

"Okay, but you know where he is now, right? The police didn't know that before. Now, you know he's in Red River. So we have a location we can give them. Even if you drive to Red River, how will you find him? Are you going to go door to door? That's not plausible," Ty cautioned, thinking like a lawyer rather than a parent.

"What if it was Darius who was missing, Ty? Or Niles? Or Zayla?" They tensed at the mere thought of it, the thought of my reality becoming theirs. "You wouldn't sit back and let the police do their jobs, and you know it. This is my son, Ty. I don't have a choice to let them handle it. If I do that, Kat and her husband could hurt him. They could...sell him. They could run away with him, and I may never see him again. I couldn't forgive myself if I didn't try my hardest to save him."

"I understand what you're saying, I do, but what I'm telling you is that it's not the same for you. You can go up to this woman's house, ask questions, sure. But Dani and I —we have to let the police do the work. We can't be involved."

"What are you talking about? I would never back down if it were your child."

"That's your privilege, Palmer. You know we'd move heaven and earth for you, we would. But we have kids to think about, too. If someone sees a black man walking around their yard uninvited, they're going to shoot me or call the police and *they* could shoot me. I may be a Harvard-educated, sharply dressed black man, but I'm still a black man. We want to help you, but not if it means doing anything that could take us away from our kids. Having us with you would put you in more danger, too. We have to think about so much more than you do, Palmer. You're a well-dressed white woman. You could walk *in* her house if you wanted and probably be fine. I couldn't walk up her driveway. Dani either. I'm sorry."

"I hadn't even thought," I said, my throat dry. Dannika had been my best friend all my life. Ty was like a brother to me. I never thought about our differences in that way. I never thought about the things they didn't talk about, the struggles I never had to see. "I'm sorry."

He huffed. "You don't have to be sorry. I don't want you to be. You didn't do anything wrong. We want to help. We do. It about kills me to say this to you now, but Dani and I have talked about it. I'm just not comfortable with this. We can't go driving up to houses at night. We can't be in neighborhoods where people don't know I'm a lawyer. If someone calls the cops on you, you may get a warning. If someone calls the cops on us, we could end up in jail, if we don't end up dead. There are amazing cops out there, don't get me wrong, but it's still a risk. It's a much bigger risk for us than you. Don't you see that? We love you, but it's a whole different world for us. We don't talk about these things because we don't want to make you uncomfortable, but that doesn't mean that every time we go to a restaurant with you, we don't feel like we're less scrutinized than when we're alone. Or when we go shopping, we don't have to make sure we keep our hands out of our pockets. I get what you want to do, Palmer. If it were my kid, I'd feel the same. The difference is, if it were my kid, I wouldn't have the option to act on those feelings. I'd have to do what I'm told or else I'd be risking leaving my kids parentless. We came with you because we feel like it's our duty to help you. We care about you. And about Gray. But this is where it ends for us as far as an investigation. You can stay with us for as long as you need, but Dani has to realize we can't help with this. I see it too much at my firm. It's too dangerous, and it's always on my mind."

I swallowed. "I understand. I'm sorry to have put you in this position."

He shook his head, meeting my eyes in the rearview, and I could tell he felt bad. Dani wouldn't look back. We rode the whole way home in silence, while I called Officer Kessler to leave an update on her voicemail.

When we got home, Dani walked with me to the bedroom, wringing her hands together. She shut the door behind her as Ty went to bed.

"He means well," she said, staring at me.

"Dani, you don't have to explain. I know he does. Ty's done so much for me. You both have. I'm sorry I put you in a dangerous position. I'd never do that on purpose. I'd never forgive myself if—"

She held up a hand, shaking her head. "There's a lawyer at Ty's firm, Owen. His husband is a cop. Ty got a call earlier that they were looking into me, just a head's up from Owen's husband, Jay."

"Looking into you? Why?"

She released a heavy breath through her nose. "Because I was with you at the marina."

"But...you had nothing to do with this."

"I know that and you know that, but some people don't need to see anything more than skin color to assume someone's guilty. Jay said they didn't find anything, but he wanted us to be aware. He's a good cop. A good guy, and we consider Owen a friend. It just really upset Ty, embarrassed him a bit, too. He...he sees so much at work, and he's always worried about us. I just...I can't go against what he says—not about this."

"I wouldn't want you to." It's my turn to pull her into a hug. "I love you so much. Thank you for going with me today. Thank you for always being with me."

When we broke apart, there were tears in her eyes. "We're going to find him, right?"

I felt tears falling down my own cheeks, and when I spoke again, it was a vow. "I won't give up until we do."

CHAPTER TWENTY-FIVE

An hour later, the house was silent. For a while after Dannika had left me to sleep, I could hear them whispering from the bedroom. I felt terrible for what I'd done, for the position I'd put them in, and for not even realizing there was a position to begin with. I wouldn't do it again. Wouldn't chance it for the world.

Instead, once the house fell silent, I scribbled a note and left it on the kitchen counter.

Dani and Ty,

Thank you for always taking care of me. I have to go find him. I can't give up, and I can't wait. I love you both. Give the babies kisses from me.

Palmer

With that, I walked out the front door and called an Uber. The black Hyundai pulled up, allowing me to climb in. The driver, Alex, offered me a bottle of water or a phone charger. I accepted both and opened my Facebook, searching for Katherine Thompson and the name of her town, praying it would pull something up. It was a small town, even smaller than Crestview, so I had to hope.

I waited as my Facebook loaded…

And continued loading…

Finally, a list of names popped up. The first three weren't her, the fourth didn't have a profile picture at all. Two of the four weren't even in our state. One had the last name River, rather than being from Red River.

I clicked 'See More' and, as soon as it loaded, I gasped.

Got you.

I'd recognize the face that had been burned into my memory any day. I clicked on her profile, watching it load, and her face filled my screen. The profile photo was her, though her hair was now a coal black rather than strawberry-blonde. When had that happened? Was this an outdated picture? I checked the date and noted that she'd just posted it the day before. So, she'd changed her look. She was definitely hiding something.

I scrolled through her page, which was mostly private, and there were no pictures of Gray. There was, however, a photo of a house with the caption **We're homeowners!**

It had been shared two years ago. I clicked on it, reading the house number: 618. There was no street name, but someone had been tagged at one point. Her husband, most likely. I ran my mouse over the picture.

Tag removed, it said, highlighting a box where his name had probably once been.

I closed out of Facebook and opened my browser, typing in her name. **Katherine Thompson Red River, NC 618**

I pressed enter, and this time, it was the top search

result, though the name on the listing made my throat go dry. A chill ran over my spine as I clicked on the link.

No.

Please God, no.

The page loaded, and I felt my pulse growing erratic as sheer black fright swept over me.

618 Melbourne Lane

Red River, NC

Property Owners: Benjamin and Katherine Lewis

Ben.

CHAPTER TWENTY-SIX

An hour later, I was pulling into Red River. I'd had the Uber driver drop me off at home just long enough to switch vehicles. I didn't have much time. I couldn't wait any longer.

I knew where my child was and, come hell or high water, I was going to get him back. I drove through the quiet streets of the tiny town, so peaceful and serene, yet holding so much evil. I still couldn't get it through my head that Ben knew—was related to, was *married* to, maybe—Kat. I didn't know how they knew each other, but I didn't care. He'd lied to me. He'd let this woman into our lives, chosen her over me, and let her take my child. If I ever saw him again, I was sure I'd kill him.

I arrived on Melbourne Lane, driving slowly. The street lights flickered above me, giving the quiet street an ominous glow, and I looked for the home that would hold my child. *Please let him be here.*

Six eighteen was the third house from the end of the dead-end street. Inside, there were lights on downstairs, but the lights upstairs were all off. I stopped the car, climbing from it and walking across the yard.

I took cautious steps, looking over my shoulder to be sure no one would see me. What if they'd sold the house? What if they were no longer the owners? What would I do then? I pushed the thoughts from my head, forcing myself to keep going.

I approached the side of the house, pressing myself against the white, metal siding and listening carefully. I could hear the low, steady drone of a television running from somewhere inside the house.

Then, a baby began to fuss, his cries carrying through the house.

I slapped a hand over my mouth, quieting the sobs that came out with no warning and no regard for my safety. *He was there.* I'd found him. I needed to get into the house.

Quick footsteps hurried across the house, and I tried to follow them, walking around the side and toward the back. I reached over the gate to unlatch it, letting myself into the back yard. From there, I lost the sound of the footsteps and fought furiously to find them. Instead, a light flicked on on the second floor, and I could see a shadow moving around. Gray's cries stopped, making me cry harder. Already, she was able to soothe him.

Or was it Ben? Ben could've been the one comforting him. How could he live with himself knowing I wasn't there? Knowing if he had his way, Gray would never know his mother. What would he tell him about me? Would he tell him anything at all? I stepped behind a bush, keeping my body close to the house as I watched the shadows cast through the yellow glow of the light upstairs.

I sank down onto the mulch of the flower bed, watching the light and feeling helpless. My child was just feet from me, and I had no way to get to him. He was crying for me, for the nourishment only I could give him, and I couldn't get there.

I should call the police. I knew it, but I couldn't. I had no proof that it was Gray inside, no proof that Kat or Ben —either one—were inside. I had to get proof. I had to know for sure.

Once the cries had gone quiet for a while, the light upstairs flipped off, and I heard the footsteps descending the stairs.

I walked through the fenced-in backyard cautiously, looking for something to spark an idea. There was an awning above the back porch that would allow me to walk straight up to the window, but I wasn't nearly tall enough to get to it. I walked up to the rusted patio set and grabbed one of the chairs. I still wasn't sure whether it would get me up there, but I had to try.

I turned the chair backward against the support beam for the awning. It groaned under my weight, and I froze, waiting, my heart so loud in my chest I thought I was going to pass out.

After a few silent moments had passed, I leaned the rest of the way up, resting my forearms against the roof. I'd need to use all of my strength, including my core, which had no strength left to give since my cesarean.

I braced myself, letting out a steady breath with my lips in the shape of an 'O,' then heaved, pulling myself up.

I cried out, unable to hold the noise in, pain ripping through my body like bolts of lightning. I was worried I'd torn open my still-healing scar, that my guts would be falling out by the time I made it to the roof, but I couldn't stop. This was my metaphorical car, and I was lifting it off of my child with every ounce of adrenaline I could muster.

I pulled, shimmying one leg up and onto the roof, then the other. When I was up, I collapsed, breathing heavily and blinking back tears. I moved a hand to my lower belly, checking to make sure my surgical scar was still closed. To my great relief, though it felt like one place may have opened up, the wound was still mostly closed and I felt no blood. I lay still for a moment, catching my breath and recovering from the intense pain before rolling over and pushing myself up. I took careful steps across the roof, hurrying to balance myself against the edge of the house and toward the window. When I got there, I lifted at the screen, removing it relatively easily. I tried to push up on the glass of the window, but it wouldn't budge.

I pushed in, then up, fighting with it. It had to open. I was so close. Just a glass-length away from him. I shoved once more and the window shook, but it wouldn't unlock.

From inside, I heard his cries again. I'm not sure if all babies' cries sound alike, but somehow, somewhere deep in my bones, I knew that was my son. I knew it had to be him, and I knew he could tell I was close. He needed me.

His cries grew louder, and I shoved away from the window, lowering myself to the roof when the light flicked on again. I heard her footsteps growing nearer, and then I heard her voice.

"What's the matter, baby? Why can't you sleep?" she cooed. Her voice was exactly how I remembered. Eerily sweet and smooth, slightly childish. It made me sick to my stomach.

Suddenly, I had an idea. I scooted toward the edge once again and stared down at the grass below. I was six feet up, and already hurt and sore, but I saw my window of opportunity. Without a second thought, I pushed off, shoving myself to the ground. I landed with a thud, tumbling onto the wet grass. I rolled over and pushed up without a second to breathe. I moved quickly across the concrete back patio and up to the door. I had one chance to make it work, and I had to pray the door was unlocked and that no one was downstairs. If Ben was there, I'd confront him. I wasn't afraid for myself, only for Gray.

I twisted the knob and shoved, and the door sprung open at once. It took a minute for me to realize I was even inside, pure shock sitting heavily on my chest. How had I managed this? I didn't have time to question it. Instead, I shut the door behind me. I was in a small, dark, and quiet kitchen, and the light from the living room was coming from straight ahead. I moved to the left, into a laundry room, and looked around. The house smelled musty and closed up, I guessed from being empty for so long. There were piles of clothes on the floor in front of the washer and an overflowing hamper in the far corner. The over-sized sink smelled of mildew and had what looked like wet cigarette butts in its drain.

I moved along the wall, following the shadows, and came to a hallway. To my right was the staircase that led upstairs—led to Gray. To my left was a door. I hurried up the stairs, taking quiet but quick steps on my way to the second floor. As soon as I took the last step, a door opened, and I saw her emerge. She had her back to me, and I darted into the door to my right before she turned around. The room was pitch black, but I didn't dare turn on any lights.

I stayed completely still, breathing heavily as I waited for her footsteps to carry on down the stairs. She was slow to go, and for a moment, I didn't hear anything. But eventually, thankfully, I heard her traveling back downstairs.

I counted to thirty, giving her time to settle in once I imagined she'd had time to arrive in the living room, and then I opened the door.

When I did, I froze. The house was dark. The television and light from downstairs had been turned off.

Where was she?

I moved to shut the door back and heard footsteps coming, returning up the stairs, and my heart pounded harder. Who was it? Just her? Or someone else? Was it Ben? The man I'd met at the house who I didn't have a name for? What if I was in her bedroom? I ran a hand along the wall, searching for a sign as to what room I was in. I connected with a light switch as I heard her growing closer but passed over it, searching for more. My hand connected with a piece of cool, flat metal. A mirror. I dropped my hands, feeling along the sticky, grimy counter. I was in a bathroom. I glided across the room as I heard someone moving at the top of the staircase and felt for a bathtub. I would hide behind the curtain if someone came in. As I made contact with the glass panes of a walk-in shower, my heart sank. There was no way I could hide there.

I panted in terror as I listened for them to open the door. To my great relief, the footsteps continued past, and I heard them carry on down the hall, farther than Gray's room. A door shut a few moments later, and I released a long, strained breath.

I sank down to the floor, waiting to give them a chance to fall asleep. If Gray were to start crying, she'd come for him. I needed to give myself the best chance possible, though my entire body tingled with excitement and anticipation. I was seconds away from holding him in my arms, and it was more exciting and terrifying than being wheeled down the long hall on my way to deliver him. This time, though, we were both in more danger.

I sank to the linoleum of the bathroom floor, smelling the ammonia of uncleaned urine on the floor, and curled my lips. My body hurt, and taking the moment to slow down was showing me just how much. My stomach wound felt like it had been torn open again, despite there being no blood, and my skin screamed in agony. My arms were so sore I was sure I'd scraped my elbow on the roof, my feet were throbbing from my fall, and I'd cut my back on the gutter on the way down. I was exhausted and terrified, but I couldn't stop. I was this close. If I'd given up, I'd never have gotten this far.

Gray was depending on me. I was all he had. I had to find him. I had to get him out of here and away from this woman...away from the danger his father put him in.

We could move away, change our names, and disappear. No one would have to know who we were or where we came from. It wasn't safe for us to stay. The thought of taking him away was bittersweet, mostly because of my career and Dannika. But I would give it all up, burn it all down for him.

When the house had been silent for a while, I pushed up from the floor and moved toward the door. I pulled it open a half inch per second, easing it until there was enough space for me to sneak out into the dark hallway. I could see moonlight seeping in under the doors as I moved stealthily down the hall. I stopped at the door that held my son, taking a half-breath to prepare myself.

This was it.

I placed one hand on the cool, metal knob, the other on the wood of the door, counted to three in my head, and pushed.

CHAPTER TWENTY-SEVEN

The small room was painted with moonlight, giving me just enough to see what it contained. The crib was in the far corner of the mostly empty room. It was old and worn, with a few of the bars painted while others weren't. There was a wicker rocking chair just beside it, piled high with a combination of musty hand-me-downs and brand new baby clothes. A picture frame hung on the wall, though there was not yet a picture in it.

I moved across the room quickly, the rough carpet rubbing against my shoes on my way to him.

I took a deep breath, my vision clouding as tears quickly filled them, then dropped down onto him before I could stop them. I reached into the crib and picked him up. He was dressed in only a diaper, his hair slick with sweat in the hot room. He'd grown so much in just a few days.

I lifted him to my chest, and he began to cry out, though he calmed at once against my skin.

He knew me.

He hadn't forgotten.

I was still his mom.

"Shhh, Gray baby," I whispered, inhaling his scent. I never wanted to lose that smell, never wanted to let him go. I was torn between standing there forever and savoring him, breaking down into sobs with gratitude at finally having him back, and running for our lives. I squeezed him tightly, kissing his head and wiping down his cheeks. "It's okay, baby. Mommy's here."

I sucked in a breath as he let out another cry, and I bounced him feverishly. My breasts filled with milk, painful and swollen at once, which only seemed to make his crying worse. Panic swept through me, my body turning to ice as I tried and failed to calm him. His body writhed in my arms, and I moved to the window, unlocking it with my free hand and attempting to lift it up.

I struggled against the heavy, painted-shut window. *Come on, come on, come on.* Gray's cries grew louder, more fury-filled, in my ear. He was hungry. He was angry. He was afraid.

Behind me, the door flew open with a gust of air, and the light flipped on. I hadn't heard her coming. I didn't know she was there. I turned around in horror, staring at the face I'd had playing on a loop through my mind for days. Her hair was dark now, just like in her most recent picture.

Her eyes narrowed at me, the knife in her hand drawn high like an ancient dagger set to be slashed through a stone.

"Put him down," she demanded, her voice low. I held up a hand, shielding him from her as she moved closer.

"Okay, okay... Don't hurt him," I begged, placing him back in the crib quickly before turning around, blocking Gray with my body.

"Palmer, right? What are you doing here?" she asked, her brow furrowed. "How did you find me?"

I shook my head. "Does it even matter? I just want him back. Let me take my baby, and I'll never tell the police where you are."

"You'll never tell them anything anyway," she said, spittle forming in the corners of her mouth. "You're never leaving here. Don't you get that, Palmer? You couldn't just leave us alone, could you? Coming here tonight was a grave mistake."

"I could never leave you alone as long as you had my son. I just want him back. Just let me take him, and I'll go away. I promise you I will."

"You could just go have another one. Don't you know how lucky you are?" she cried, her hand shaking as she tightened her grip on the knife.

"It doesn't have to be this way," I said, shaking my head. "I just want my son. Please. I can't be without him."

"You really don't get it. He's my son now. Mine. He's not going home with you. He's going to forget about you. He's not going to ever know you existed."

"Why?" I cried, turning as she moved around the room, always keeping my body between hers and the crib. "Why are you doing this?"

"He was never yours! He was supposed to be mine! He was supposed to be mine!" she fumed, her frail body shaking as it grew red with anger. I watched as she lowered the knife just a hair, trying to decide if I could catch her off guard and wrangle it from her grasp.

"He's not, though, Katherine. He's my son. He needs me—"

She lunged forward, and I put my hand up, grasping her wrist as she attempted to plunge the knife into my chest. I pushed back, my strength an even match for hers, even at my weakest. I shoved her, trying to grasp the knife, but she pulled it back, kicking me square in the stomach. I fell to my knees, my arms wrapped around myself as I crawled away from her, trying to catch my breath. Something was wrong. My stomach felt strange, red hot with pain. When I glanced down, there was blood on my shirt. She moved forward with purpose, grabbing hold of my hair, and I grasped the nearest thing I could find, a lamp on the nightstand next to the crib, and swiped it at her, every movement a white-hot poker to my stomach. She met my arm with the knife, slicing into my skin, and I dropped the lamp. "Ah!" I cried out, trying to get closer to the crib again. I couldn't allow her to touch my baby again.

I darted past her, ignoring the pain in my stomach, and she spun around, her arm raised high in the air as she plunged the knife down. One of my hands was pinned underneath me, supporting my weight, the other now carrying a deep, knife gash, and I found it impossible to move it quick enough. I watched in slow motion as the knife came down, waiting for the blow. I ducked, heard the slam of the door as it swung open and slammed into the wall, and watched the feet approaching just as the knife connected with my shoulder, the new pain competing with the old. I screamed out, jerking back and looking up as the pain tore through my body, and I collapsed on the musty carpet.

When I looked up, the woman stood above me, but rather than triumph on her face, there was pain. Confusion. She looked down to where, on the center of her pink shirt, a violet circle grew. She dropped the knife, stepping backward. I gasped as I watched her fall, the pain in my stomach throbbing as my vision faded in and out, and I reached a hand around to staunch the bleeding from my shoulder.

I looked back to the doorway, still not believing what I saw. He stood in the doorway, a large, bloody kitchen knife in his hand as he towered over her body with a terrifying grimace. He was bleeding from his head and upper thigh, and completely covered in dirt. When he looked at me, his expression softened, even underneath the mud.

"Ben?"

CHAPTER TWENTY-EIGHT

BEN

I was never going to be the hero in this story. I made too many mistakes. Did all the wrong things. But I wasn't the monster she thought I was.

I still remembered everything about the day I got the call. What I was wearing—white shirt, blue tie, black slacks. What I was thinking about just before—whether or not our boss would make us stay late because her customer was being extra difficult. What I had for lunch—tacos that I threw up the second the call ended.

I remembered seeing the number pop up on my screen, one I didn't recognize. I shouldn't have answered it, and normally I wouldn't on the clock, but I had to then. Something pulled me to it, some unexplainable force.

I remembered the way the words ran over me, like blades piercing my skin steady and slow. "Your wife was in a car accident. We need you to meet us at Saint Francis."

I stood from the desk, my knees colliding with its wood. "Is she...is she okay?"

The voice was quiet. "It doesn't look good, son. Just meet us soon."

I hung up, emptied my stomach into the wastebasket, and rushed out the door without a word to anyone. To be honest, I didn't remember the drive there. It was all kind of a blacked-out part of my memory, but I remembered the rest in such vivid color, it was as if there was no space left for that insignificant part of the day.

The hospital was full of nurses and patients, busy like bees, and I somehow found my way to the front desk and demanded to see her. They made me wait for hours, believing the worst. Believing she was dead.

That I'd lost her.

When the doctor finally came for me, he pulled his scrub cap down in front of his chest, his expression a full apology without a word.

"She's being taken to the ICU. She came through surgery...she's not in the clear yet, but we believe she's going to pull through."

I swallowed, rubbing my palm over my face, mixing my sweat with my tears. "Thank God," I choked out. "Is she..." I blinked. "I mean...the baby. Is the baby okay?"

The doctor's eyes fell. "I'm so sorry. Your wife suffered extreme trauma to her abdomen in the crash. We did all we could to save them both, but we lost the baby's heartbeat. Because of all the damage, there was no way to repair her uterus. We were forced to do a total hysterectomy." He put a hand on my shoulder. "She's going to need you when she wakes up. Not only did she lose a baby today, she lost the chance to ever have one again."

I could see it in his expression...she'd never recover.

Not really. Even though she'd healed physically, the bleeding stopped, her scars faded, the woman I'd married was not the woman I was living with anymore.

Over time, we grew apart. I know it's cliché. I know you're thinking about what a piece of shit I am right now, and believe me, I am too. But how do you help someone who doesn't want to be helped? How can you be there for someone who shuts you out?

After a year of silence, a year of direct answers to direct questions, a year of doctor's appointments and crying, and endless fights and blame and drinking too much and not eating enough, I couldn't do it anymore.

In my weakest moment, I asked her for a divorce. I walked away from the girl I loved, the girl I'd loved since high school, the girl I'd thought I'd love for the rest of my life, and when I did…I felt free for the first time in so long.

I never completely allowed myself to feel my own grief because I was always deescalating hers. I never felt allowed to get mad, even when she'd left the food out all night and it spoiled, even when she'd quit her job and left everything up to me, even when she refused to see the doctors I couldn't afford but tried to get her to see anyway.

She needed help, but I was out of options. I was out of patience, out of pain, out of grace.

Her parents checked her into a facility to deal with her depression, but she checked out almost immediately. She refused to be helped.

I'm not blaming her, okay? I know I'll never know the way it felt to have a life taken from my body, but I lost my son that day, too. I lost the family I planned. The future I predicted. I lost everything I thought my future would hold in the blink of an eye, but I stayed. I tried to get better. Get over it. I tried to make things better for her, show her there were other ways. We could still have a family. There were options.

She wasn't interested.

So, believe me when I say I exhausted every avenue I believed I had. I tried. God, I tried. In the end, it wasn't enough. *I* wasn't enough. She wanted our child back, and I could never give her that.

No one could.

I met Palmer the month after I moved from Red River to Oceanside. When I say she was not in the plan, I mean it more than I can tell you. I wanted to clear my head, figure out what I wanted for my life, figure out how to deal with all I'd dealt with over the last year. So, I left the bank. I got a job at a hardware store, just trying to make ends meet while I crashed on a buddy's couch, and I vowed to move on with my life.

When Palmer came into the store one day, looking for wood to build her own bookshelf, I asked her out before I'd even realized it happened. I legitimately don't even remember how it happened. Two weeks later, I finished the bookshelf she'd given up on when her Pinterest plan didn't work out.

Three months later, three blissful months spent with someone who actually wanted me around, someone who could look me in the eye and not see all the pain my love had caused, someone whose entire history with me wasn't torn to shreds by a drunk idiot running a red light, and I couldn't get enough. I lapped her up like a dog to water. Breathed her in like she was oxygen I'd never had. I fell in love with her harder than I could've braced myself for, and when she told me she was pregnant, I proposed right away. Like, that second.

It wasn't because of the baby, though that certainly helped. It was almost like I'd been waiting for an excuse to do it. I loved her, but I didn't want to scare her off. She was fiercely independent, wealthy on her own, used to doing things her way. She didn't need me, and that terrified me. I didn't want to move things too fast and scare her away.

It wasn't until after we announced Palmer's pregnancy that I heard from Kat for the first time since I'd filed for the divorce. She'd been refusing to sign the papers, but once she heard about the baby, I begged her to sign. I wanted to marry Palmer. Kat wanted proof that it was mine. She was angry, hurt. I hadn't told Palmer about my past, so I could never explain the need for a paternity test to her. I ordered a fake paternity test result online from a prank store and had it sent to her. A week later, she signed the papers. I thought it would be the last time I heard from her.

When Palmer was midway through her pregnancy, Kat contacted me again. She apologized, said she was sorry for the way she'd handled things. The way she handled everything. She told me she was healthy. That she'd been going to therapy, processing her grief. She'd started her old food blog back up, and she was getting to travel around the US to run it. She told me she was sorry for all the pain she put me through and that she knew I'd tried my best.

She told me that she loved me. That she always would.

Without me having to say it, she knew I felt the same way.

As the pregnancy neared its end, Kat would send me occasional congratulations and warm wishes. I never believed it was inappropriate. After Gray was born, she asked if she could meet him. She said that seeing me happy, seeing me moving on, me as a dad, she thought it could help her move on as well. She said she was thinking about adopting.

I was an idiot. I remembered her for who she was, believed her when she said she was better. I met her at the park near our apartment on Palmer's first day back to work. I never wanted to hide what I was doing—I didn't want to sneak around—but I couldn't bear to tell Palmer about Kat. I didn't want her to think about me, what I still thought of myself—that I was a coward. That I ran away when things got hard. That I wasn't worthy of love if I couldn't stick around and make my vows mean something. I could never tell her the truth. I didn't want her to look at me the way my family did. The way Kat's family did.

The first time we met up, she seemed so normal. Like her old self. I was cautious with Gray, but I let her talk to him, let her play with him. It really seemed like it helped. She even brought him a sweet little onesie that was quirky and adorable, just like her. I thought things were going to be okay. Finally, this nagging worry in the back of my head could fade because it genuinely seemed like she was better.

That night, her father called me. I hadn't heard from him since I'd left, though since then, I'd been sending him most of my paychecks—one thousand dollars a month—to help get the house paid off that Kat and I bought together. He had moved Kat home to Crestview; she was living in her parents' rental house next door to them, but the mortgage still had to be paid until it would sell. In a small town, that could be awhile. It was costing me nearly everything I made to do it, but it was only fair. The divorce had granted it to her, but I still felt responsible. It wasn't her fault she'd struggled to keep a job, nor her parents' fault. They weren't rich, and they'd always struggled to make ends meet, so taking on our mortgage wasn't exactly ideal for them. We all just shouldered the responsibility the best way we knew how.

When he called that night, he was furious. And I had no idea why. He asked what I was thinking seeing Kat again, that she'd been working to get better, but that seeing me caused her to spiral.

I felt like shit, okay? I mean, how was I supposed to know she'd been lying all that time. I'd gone back to following her blog, and she really did seem to be her old self again. I had no idea how far the lie had gone. Apparently she'd been telling everyone in Crestview that we were still married, that I was away for work, and her most recent lie—the reason her dad was calling me then...she was claiming we were planning to adopt a baby.

At hearing that, I should've never gone back. I should've protected my child above all else, but Kat was my first best friend. She was the person I watched grow from a mud-covered four-year-old to a beautiful bride on our wedding day. She's the one I cried with when my sister died. The one whose hand I held when my parents announced their divorce. Growing up, we spent every waking minute together. I'd abandoned her once, I just…I couldn't do it again.

We made a plan. I was going to see her again, to try and smooth things over, explain what was happening and make sure everything was okay. I thought things went okay. With me, she was totally normal. She said she understood that we weren't together, that she was only lying to save face, but she knew she had to tell the truth.

When she texted me and told me Palmer was in Crestview, I panicked. I didn't know if it was even true. I didn't know what she was doing there or what Kat would do. What Kat would tell her. I lied about the break-in, pretended to be panicked to get Palmer home, get her away from my ex-wife at all costs. I used a fork to break off a bit of the trim. It was stupid, I know, but we'll just chalk it up to yet another dumb decision I made on the long list I'm sharing with you. It's far from the worst.

When her dad called again, he said they were going to move her back in with them. They said it wasn't safe to have her living alone anymore. She'd been erratic, missing all hours of the day and night, blowing through money, sleeping outside on the patio. They were terrified she was going to spiral further, and they wanted to act quickly. I was just supposed to keep her busy while they hired movers to empty her house and get it set up in theirs. It was only one day. He asked me to take her out to dinner one more time, to keep her busy because she had no one else, and then to never speak to her again.

I thought it was the least I could do, honestly. I felt I owed it to them. To her. We went to eat somewhere crowded and public, like before, but she was agitated. Angry. She complained about her fight with her father. Complained about her food blogging. Complained about everything. She kept wanting to go home, but it was too early. Her father had asked me to keep her gone until mid-afternoon.

When she insisted, I went with her. If I could go back and change that, I would. If I could redo anything in my life, it would be that moment. That stupid, foolish, blind moment when I thought there was no way she could ever hurt me.

She was sick.

She was sad.

She was a lot of things.

But she wasn't evil.

We went back to her house, and I insisted we go outside. With just a bit of a heads up, her dad had the movers take a lunch break. Luckily, he'd only had the bedrooms cleared out thus far, so I ushered her through the living room and kitchen before she could notice anything.

When I came outside and saw her trying to nurse my son, I nearly lost it. I knew then how far gone she was. If she hadn't had Gray in her arms, I would've bolted. I would've thrown a fit. But how could I do that when I didn't know what she was capable of? I didn't know how far she'd fallen.

After I'd given her the bottle to feed him, I told her we had to go. Told her we had somewhere to be. Instead, I drove around the block, then parked next door at her parents' house and told them what had happened. I told them how sorry I was, but I couldn't help them anymore. They were on their own. I told them I'd continue to pay on the Red River mortgage, but that was it. I couldn't put my wife and my son in danger. I saw it in their eyes then, it was just one more thing I was disappointing them on, but I couldn't help it.

When I left their house, I buckled Gray in and walked around to my side of the car.

As soon as I sat down, the back door opened and shut, and I met her eyes in the rearview.

"What the—"

Something heavy smacked into my head with force.

Then it all went black.

CHAPTER TWENTY-NINE

BEN

When I came to, I'd been shoved over to the passenger's side of my car. I wasn't buckled in and wasn't even really in the seat. Kat was driving, her eyes wide and maniacal. I screamed at her, my head pounding with every bump. I asked her to pull the car over, told her she didn't really want this. I tried everything to get her to stop. Tried everything to get her to choose a different path.

Despite it all, that's my biggest regret. Because she could've had a good life. She should've. She deserved better.

I remember smelling fish and saltwater when she stopped the car, my vision still blurry from my throbbing head. When I pulled down the visor to get a good look, there was a nasty gash on my forehead.

She was wearing my ball cap, and I watched as she climbed from the car, taking the keys with her. We were at the marina, but I couldn't figure out why. I watched her saunter across the yard to the boat rental shack. She approached a group of guys, no one I knew, and handed them something that I couldn't see.

I couldn't worry about what she was doing. I had to act. It may have been my only chance. I got out of the car and shut my door carefully, lowering myself to the ground and crawling back toward Gray's door. I stood up, pulling at the handle at the same time I heard the locks click.

She'd locked him in.

I pulled at the handle wildly, looking over the car to where she stood in the distance with my fob held in the air, a stern expression on her face. I pulled on the car door so hard the whole thing shook, trying to figure out how to break the window. It was ninety degrees and my son was locked in the car.

I slammed my elbow into it, which led to pain and nothing else, before she approached the car again, walking to block Gray's door. "Do you want to come with us, or no?"

I looked to the group of guys, who were jogging off toward the lake, no idea what she was talking about. "Us who?"

"Not them," she said with a scowl. "Gray and me. Do you want to go with us?"

"What are you talking about? You can't take him anywhere. He needs to go home, Kat." I tried to reason with her, to find the sane woman I'd loved not so long ago, but she was gone. Her eyes were empty and cold. "He needs to go home with me. To see his mother." I spoke slowly, hoping to bring her back to reality. As much as I could see the madness, I still wanted to believe she was who I wanted her to be.

"Don't you understand?" she asked, storming back around to the driver's side of the car. "*I'm* his mother now, Ben." She put the key in the door, unlocking just hers and climbed in, starting it up. My life flashed before my eyes as I pictured her driving away with Gray. I pounded on the window with all my might.

"Let me in! Kat, don't do this. Please don't do this. Come on, Kat. *Please! Please!*" My voice grew high and desperate, attracting the eyes of a few passersby, but she just stared at me with a smug expression. Finally, she unlocked the door, and I jerked it open in a second. I sank down in the seat. My door wasn't even closed before she whipped around and drove away.

"Where are you taking us?" I said, almost afraid to ask.

She looked at me, a mad twinkle in her eye that made me swallow audibly. "Don't you know? We're going home."

I stared straight ahead and watched as she turned on the road, not headed toward Crestview, but toward Red River. I needed to text her parents, to text Palmer, to call the police. We needed help, and I wasn't sure what help I could be. I reached in my back pocket slowly, sneaking my hand across the side of the seat.

"You won't find it," she said, obviously spying what I was attempting.

She reached in her bra, pulling out my wallet and phone and waving them around.

"What the hell? Why do you have those?" I asked.

"You don't need them anymore," she said, then laughed

loudly. "We're all you need, Bennie Boo-Boo. Our family is back together. I can't thank you enough for that."

I stared straight ahead as the car began to gain speed, my heart thudding in my chest.

What had I done?

What had I done?

CHAPTER THIRTY

BEN

By the time we pulled into the Red River house's driveway, Gray was having a fit. He was hot and hungry, and I had just a few bags of milk left. How long would they last us? A few days, maybe? How long would it be until I could get away from her?

"I should probably take him and get formula," I said. "That'll give you time to get his room ready."

"Do you honestly think I'm an idiot?" she asked, rolling her eyes. "I'm going to nurse him. It's better for the baby."

"You don't have milk—"

She slammed her hand on the center console. *I'm going to nurse him!*"

She climbed from the car, taking the keys with her. I reached to the back, touching his hand. "It's okay, Gray," I told him, knowing it was mostly a lie. I had to make it okay, but I had no idea how. She opened the back door, reaching for him, and I shot out of the car and hurried to her side. "Kat, if you're going to do this, we have to take care of him. He needs formula. He has to eat."

She stalked past me, carrying my screaming child as every bit of my insides screamed for me to save him. But how? She led me up to the house and pulled a set of keys from her pocket, unlocking the door. I needed to get my phone back. I needed to call for help. I wouldn't leave Gray with her.

She took him in the living room, the musty house so familiar, yet so different. Had I really been happy here once? With this woman who held such a darkness? I missed Palmer more than I could say. I ached for her, for her warmth, for her brain. She would know what to do, how to save our son.

I was not sure I could ever face her again, even after I got him out of this. Would she ever forgive me?

I followed her as she laid him on the couch. "I think he needs a diaper change." She looked at me. "Can I trust you to stay here while I get a diaper?"

I swallowed. "Of course."

She turned away from us, not looking entirely sure, and I heard her footsteps ascend the stairs in the hall. I scooped Gray up without a warning and darted from the living room, through the kitchen, and out the back door. I held him close to my chest as he screamed, running around the corner of the house.

I stopped in my tracks, staring at her as she cut me off, coming around the side of the house. She held a large shovel in her hands.

"You should've done what you promised, Ben."

"What did I promise?"

"You promised to love me, to take care of me in sickness and in health. Then you left me."

I swallowed, rubbing a hand over Gray's back. "Kat, I'm...I'm so sorry."

"Sorry doesn't fix this, Ben. It doesn't fix me. I *needed* you. I needed you the most, and you walked away and started over with someone new. Someone better."

"I didn't know what to do, Kat. I was scared. I was terrified I was just making it worse for you—"

"And when I saw her at the hair appointment, I knew what she must think of me. I knew she believed she'd won, but I had to win. I had to win."

"There's nothing to win, Kat. Please, just let us go. You don't have to do this. You don't have to hurt us. Please..." I took a step back, and she raised the shovel. "You don't want this."

"You should've just killed me when you had the chance," she said, shaking her head with tears in her eyes.

"I don't want to—"

"*Put him down,*" she screamed.

"I don't—"

"*Now*, Ben. Before I hurt you both."

I kissed Gray's head, laying him down on the grass, and took a step toward Kat, ready to take the shovel from her. "Come on, now, let's talk this th—"

I never got to finish my sentence because at that exact moment, she swung.

After that, there was only darkness.

CHAPTER THIRTY-ONE

BEN

When my eyes opened, there was only darkness. Darkness like I'd never seen before, with not a hint of light anywhere. A clump of something heavy and moist sat in my mouth. *Gray? Where was Gray?*

Panic.

What was happening?

Ice-cold fear flooded through my veins at lightning speed.

Where was I? What had happened? I tried to sit up, tried to shove myself free, but I couldn't move. I was frozen in place, kept there by some invisible force. It was heavy and thick, a texture I didn't recognize at first. I'd been placed inside of something. Under something. I couldn't tell.

I inhaled, and the thick clump moved further down my throat. I couldn't breathe. My body flailed and convulsed, trying to free itself as my mind went to a flash of bright light.

Was I going to die right then and there? In some

KIERSTEN MODGLIN

unrecognizable place? Alone and cold? There didn't seem to be any other options.

I panicked, trying to cough and struggle against the force holding me down. *What is happening? What is happening? What is happening?* I fought through the cobwebs of my nightmare-filled memory.

Finally, my hand wriggled free, moving through something thick and unrelenting to touch my face. At first it didn't register what was happening. Where I was. How I'd gotten there. What I needed to do. Then, all at once, realization slammed into my chest. I realized where I was and what was happening. I knew who had put me there.

I knew I was going to die.

With as much force as I could muster, I shoved my hands upward, roaring through the mud in my mouth and throat. I fought through a thick layer of the moist, wet earth, and then my hands were free. Like a zombie from the grave, my hands tore through the earth to reach the fresh air above. Was my assailant still there?

I didn't care. Couldn't. I was free. I felt the cool night air on my skin as I pushed myself to sit up, coughing and spewing mucus-covered soil from my mouth.

I looked around me at the fresh dirt that was meant to be my grave. The night air was cool, and there were no stars in the sky. No light to be seen, and yet, still somehow the air was lighter than being underground. I stood up, dusting myself off. The dirt was caked into my teeth, my nails, my clothes, my hair. I was walking proof monsters existed. If I came upon me in the woods, I'd run.

I spit again, trying to free my mouth of the sour,

bloody taste of the dirt, and brush the mud from my hair. Where was I? Which direction should I go?

I had no idea. No idea about any of it. No idea how I got there or where *there* was. I reached up and touched my scalp, then jerked my hand back in agonizing pain. When I pulled my hand away, warm, sticky blood coated my palm. Though I couldn't see it clearly in the darkness, I knew what it was. I put my fingers to my scalp again, feeling the open wound just above my temple. A piece of skin hung over, so loose I could've pulled it off if it didn't sting so badly.

I tried to take a step forward, but pain tore through my body, my nerves on high alert. *What happened to me?*

I ran my hands along my body, down my thigh, and realized it was just as painful, just as wet with blood, but from a different wound. I hobbled forward, brushing dirt from my eyes and mouth with every painful step. It hurt. It all burned and throbbed and ached. Every part of me. I couldn't seem to remember anything, my mind a dark, foggy mess of fuzzy memories. What was real and what wasn't? What had I done? What had led me to an early, yet ultimately ineffective grave?

Who tried to kill me?

The last thing I remembered was…*her.* I remembered the fight at the house in Red River. I remembered learning the truth about her, about how bad she'd gotten. I remembered confronting her, begging her to let us go. Remembered it all coming together for me at once. I remembered the pain, the shovel coming down on my head. I vaguely remembered another car ride, her singing to Gray as she buried me in the dirt. The shovel piercing my thigh as she broke through the dirt and into my skin.

Pain.

Physical and emotional. All of it. At the thought, lightning-sharp pain shot through me, and I hobbled and cried and gasped for air as my lungs worked to free the mud from my sticky throat. I bent over, my body rigid with pain and trepidation as I coughed, then winced, coughed then winced. *Where was Gray? What had she done? What had I done?*

I tasted blood then, and I wondered if it was coming from my head or somewhere else entirely. How else had I been hurt? What had I been through? It was coming back to me slowly, as if I were scraping mud from the memories right along with the rest of my body.

The woods were quiet all around me, but as I made it a bit further, I saw the first sign of light. The moon lit up the night sky above me, giving me glimpses of the forest around me.

The trees were thick, the earth foggy, and my head painful. So, so much pain. I couldn't think straight, couldn't move. I should've looked over the gravesite closer for an explanation as to how I got there, but I had no way to see it and no desire to go back. Whoever put me there obviously believed I was dead, and I knew who it was. *Her.* I could see the memories more vividly now. I was sure they were real.

She'd had enough of me getting in her way, she realized I wasn't going to go along with her insane plan, and she decided to end it. To end me. I was never what she wanted. It was always Gray. The replacement for the baby she'd lost. But she wasn't going to do away with me so easily. I wasn't going down without a fight. I would save my son if it was the last thing I did.

I saw the road then, up ahead, and I forced myself forward. Each step was agonizing, each breath like a scalding dagger to the stomach. I stepped down into the ditch and out of the woods, and then back up the embankment and toward the road. *I must look like a nightmare; who would ever stop for me?*

To my surprise, someone did. The dark truck pulled to a stop next to me, and the man in the driver's seat leaned over as he rolled the window down, taking in my appearance. He was old, haggard, worn. The truck smelled of cigarettes and chewing tobacco.

"Do you need some help?" he asked. Question of the century. I obviously had a genius on my hands.

"Yes. Please."

He reached over further, pushing the door open. He wasn't afraid of me. Even bloody and covered in dirt, I didn't appear to be a threat. It must be why I went down so easily. But I felt like I'd been reborn, and I wouldn't be so easy to take down the next time.

I was coming for what was mine. I would take my son back. Go home to my wife. I would fix this somehow. I had to.

I climbed into the truck, the pain of each movement unrelenting. It hurt. It all just...hurt.

He pulled out a cell phone. "Do you want me to call an ambulance? The police?" He swallowed as he stared at me, apparently more afraid now.

"Thank you, but I'll be okay. Can you just take me

home?" I asked. My voice was gravelly and unfamiliar. How long had it been since I used it? How long had it been since she buried me? Since she thought she killed me?

I would be okay, just as soon as I ended this once and for all. I couldn't do that if the police were involved. I might have to kill her, and I had to accept that.

He nodded, his hands shaking as he moved to put the car into drive. "What happened to you?"

I didn't answer him because I didn't know. Not really. I had no idea what happened to get me to this place. I stared out the window, my body roaring with agony, and all I could think of was how I let myself get here. How I let her ruin my life.

When we reached the street, I told him to drop me off a few houses away from hers. I didn't want to give her any warning I was coming. It was suspicious, but, truth be told, I think he was glad to be rid of me. He stopped and wished me well, and I climbed from the car slowly.

I froze when I saw her car. *Palmer.*

Had she managed to find him? Managed to figure it out?

If Kat hurt either of them, I'd never forgive myself.

I pushed forward, running as fast as my leg would carry me, thick blood dripping down my thigh. When I reached the house, I heard screaming. Palmer's. Kat's. Gray was crying. I shoved open the back door and tore open a drawer, grabbing the biggest knife I could find and hurrying up the stairs.

If they weren't making so much noise, they'd know I

was coming. My footsteps were anything but quiet. Every time I stepped on my right side, I fell into the wall.

I shoved open the door and took in the scene. Palmer was on the floor, her stomach stained with blood. A dark-haired Kat stood above her, ready to attack. I didn't think twice, launching forward with the knife. It connected with her lower back, near her kidneys, and I pushed it through with force. She quivered, freezing, and I jerked it back out. It took much more force to get out than it had going in.

I sucked in a breath, still unable to process what I'd done. Kat sighed, mumbled something, then fell.

I stared down at Palmer, who looked pale and sickly. Did she hate me? Should she?

I felt too faint to know the answer. I looked back at Kat's body. A body, a woman, I'd loved with all my heart.

What did you do?

What did he do to you?

As long as I lived, I'd never forgive the driver who ran the red light and brought us to that moment.

CHAPTER THIRTY-TWO

PALMER

I stared up at Ben as he pressed his hands into my shoulder. Gray screamed from his crib behind me, and my eyes watered with pain, joy, and confusion.

"Don't move." He pulled his shirt off, wrapping it around my shoulder to staunch the bleeding.

"I...I don't understand." I panted. "I thought you...why did you..."

"Shhh," he whispered, wiping the hair that stuck to my forehead out of my eyes. "It's okay. I'll explain everything to you soon. I'll tell you everything."

I looked to where Kat was slumped on the floor. "Is she..."

He gave a stiff nod. "I couldn't chance it again. I'm sorry, Palmer. I'm so sorry."

"Check Gray. Is he okay?" I asked, wincing.

He didn't have to be told twice, standing up slowly and lifting our son from the crib. He bent down next to me again with Gray in his arms. "Do you have your phone? I need to call an ambulance."

I nodded. "My back pocket."

As he reached for it, we heard the downstairs doors open and a parade of footsteps headed our way. Kessler was one of the first in the door, her gun drawn. She took in the scene, pointing the gun at Ben.

"Palmer, you okay?" she asked.

"It's okay," I assured her. "Ben saved me. He saved Gray."

She looked uneasy and kicked the knife even further away from him, shouting down the hall. "We need a medic up here. Now." She bent down next to me, examining my shoulder, but keeping a close eye on Ben. "Are you okay?"

"I'm okay… She stabbed my shoulder. Check Gray. Take care of Gray." She held out her arms for my son, and as the EMTs arrived, she handed him off. They reappeared a few seconds later for me, putting me on a stretcher and carrying me down the hall.

"How did you get here?" I called out to Kessler before I was too far down the hall. "How did you know where we were?"

"Your friend Ty called me. He was worried about you and said you'd gone missing," she said. "We tracked your phone, saw your car, and followed the trail of blood." She pointed to the ground where there was indeed a thick trail of blood left behind by Ben.

I winced, a searing pain shooting through my shoulder. "Is Gray okay?" I asked the EMT, a young, blonde woman with incredibly white teeth. "My baby? Is he okay?"

"He looks a little hot. A little hungry. But they're giving him a thorough exam now."

Ben began to follow us, but Kessler stopped him, her face stern. I wasn't sure what to think. He'd lied to me about so much, things I didn't even know about, things I may never. But he also saved me. He saved Gray. I couldn't discount that.

I laid my head back on the stretcher, feeling dizzy as we headed out the door. I'd never been so thankful for fresh air in my life.

As we reached the stretcher and they removed the makeshift bandage Ben had made with his shirt, my head fell back, too heavy to lift it any longer. Then, whether from blood loss or exhaustion, sleep found me, and I welcomed it like an old friend.

CHAPTER THIRTY-THREE

PALMER

I woke up in the hospital with Ben by my side. He had Gray in his arms. I tensed at the sight, though his smile grew wide when he met my eyes.

"You're awake."

"What's going on?" I asked, still foggy from all that had happened.

"You're going to be fine. You lost a lot of blood. Your shoulder wasn't terrible, but you'd reopened your incision and bled quite a bit internally because of it. They said you took a pretty bad blow to your stomach."

I scoffed, adjusting myself the best that I could. "A few, actually. Can I hold him?" I held my arms out, happiness swelling inside me.

"Yeah, of course." He placed him in my arms.

I looked down at my son, his lips curling into a happy, contented smile. "Did they check him out?"

"He's perfectly healthy," Ben assured me. "He was well fed and taken care of. His diapers had been changed and everything."

"Are...you okay?" I asked, remembering his wounds.

"I'm fine, just a few stitches and some antibiotics," he said, gesturing toward his head and leg. "I'll be on crutches for a while until the muscles heal."

I nodded, suddenly in pain again, though it felt more emotional than physical. "Were you cheating on me...with her?"

His eyes widened, and he reached for my hand. "No, Palmer. No. I promised you I'd never cheat on you, and I meant it."

"Then who was she?" I asked, holding Gray closer as tears formed in my eyes.

"We don't have to do this now..."

"Yes, yes, we do."

"She was my wife."

"Before me?"

"Yes."

"And what did she want with my son?"

"Kat wasn't...she wasn't well. We lost a baby in a really traumatic way. She was thirty-six weeks along when it happened. We already knew we were having a boy. We'd already picked out a name. She...she never really recovered."

I bit down on my tongue. "That's why you divorced?"

"Mostly, yes. We grew apart. I don't...I don't really know how couples survive losses like that. I wished we could've, but we just couldn't seem to make it work."

"And you...what? You stayed in touch?"

"No," he said quickly. "No. I didn't talk to her at all until after we announced our pregnancy. She reached out to me, and I felt I owed her kindness at the very least.

When you experience something like that with someone, even when it pulls you apart, it also bonds you."

"So, then, why did she take Gray?"

"She believed Gray was her child, I think. She wanted so badly to have a baby to replace the one we lost, but we could never have afforded an adoption, even during our best times." He paused. "I tried so hard to save him, Palmer. I know it doesn't make what I did okay, but I never thought she was dangerous. She wanted to meet him. To see my child. I didn't think there was any harm, but I was wrong. I'd done so much wrong by her, I just wanted to do the right thing, and I nearly lost everything I cared about because of it."

"Were you taking a boat ride together? Why did you rent a boat?"

"I didn't. From what the police have said, and what I can remember, she had some random guys from the marina rent it in my name. She took my wallet, my ID, and my cap to make it happen. The police tracked them down and they said she gave them one hundred dollars to get in the boat and abandon it in the ocean. They hopped on a friend's boat and let it drift to shore."

"She wanted me to believe you were dead," I said softly.

He nodded.

"What about the flight?"

He chewed his lip, shaking his head. "Officer Kessler told me she booked a flight. They still think it was a diversion to get you to believe I'd left you, if you didn't believe that I was dead. I honestly don't know." He scratched his forehead. "I wish I could've understood her better."

"Did you…kill her? Is she gone?"

He nodded slowly. "I couldn't let her hurt you."

I sighed. "I don't know if I can forgive you, Ben. This is…I could've lost Gray forever."

His eyes fell to the floor. "I know. Believe me I do. I would've never forgiven myself. I still haven't—"

I touched his hand, stopping him. "But thank you. For saving me."

He smiled, and it was melancholy and pensive, the same as mine. It was what I could offer him at the time. Nothing more, nothing less. We were in this together, but it didn't mean we'd stay together. It didn't mean I forgave him or that I trusted him anymore. He'd hurt me in so many ways, and I wasn't sure I'd ever be ready to let him back into my life.

I'd learn. I'd figure it out.

But what I was learning more than anything was that letting anyone close to you was dangerous.

I stared down at my son, brushing my finger across his forehead. *Maybe it'll just be me and you against the world, little guy.*

Maybe that wouldn't be such a bad thing.

CHAPTER THIRTY-FOUR

PALMER

TWO YEARS LATER

"Grant Anderson called," Howie told me. "He wants to see those quarterly reports."

I shook my head, staring out across our brand new, expansive and incredibly bare office. It was a big upgrade on the cramped building we'd been in the first year.

"Tell Mr. Anderson that I said he's a silent partner for a reason," I told him, only half-joking. "He'll get the reports when we send them."

I stood as Dannika entered the building, her arms spread wide, mouth agape. "Girl, have you seen who's outside?"

"Who?" I asked.

"Oh, no. We're gonna need to barricade the doors and windows. It's *Nate!*" She sat her bags down, watching me.

My jaw dropped with shock. "Are you serious? What's he doing here?"

"I don't know. I hurried my happy ass inside when I

saw him. What do you want Howie to do?" she asked, grabbing a bag of chips from her purse and popping one in her mouth.

Howie scowled. "Me? I'm not security!"

I giggled. "Okay, calm down. I'm fine, guys. Honestly. If there's one thing in this world I'm no longer concerned with, it's Nate Creswell." I walked across the room, my heels clicking on the floor.

Two months after the Kat ordeal, Dannika and I had finally opened up our firm, bringing Howie along with us. It was the happiest I'd been in a long time. Gray was happy and healthy, and his doctors didn't believe he'd be affected in the slightest by all he'd gone through. He was too young and blissfully unaware.

Ben and I were working through our issues with monthly counseling. We'd started dating again, but he'd moved out and gotten his own place. We shared custody of Gray, but I had no intentions of filing for divorce. Despite all we'd gone through, I wanted to work on us. I believed Ben cared for me. I knew he cared for Gray. I just wanted to give myself time to process.

Ty's phone call had saved my life. The doctors said if the EMTs hadn't arrived when they did, I might not have made it. I'd never be able to thank him enough for that.

The house Ben and Kat owned finally sold, and Ben paid me back in full for the money he'd borrowed, even though most of it was his own, apologizing profusely for letting it get so out of hand.

I'd gone through something so terrible, something I wouldn't wish on anyone, but I'd grown stronger because of it. I had stronger friendships, a stronger bond with my son. I'd faced my fears and finally taken the leap with my business.

After going through something like I did, nothing could really seem so scary in comparison.

I pushed open the door to our building, narrowing my gaze at Nate. Two years ago, I would've cried or walked away. I never would've faced him. Now, I was a new woman.

"What are you doing here?"

His chest rose and fell with a heavy breath. "I, um, hi, first of all." He stepped closer, and I felt my stomach turn a flip. He'd always been able to do that to me. "I heard you opened up your firm. Congratulations."

"How'd you hear?"

"I've been...keeping tabs on you, Palm." He sighed, rubbing a hand across his chin.

"What are you doing here, Nate?" I pressed.

He frowned. "There's no easy way to say this, but you deserve to hear it. I'm sorry—"

I pursed my lips, holding up a hand. "Oh, you don't have to—"

"No, I do. I really do. I'm sorry for hurting you and for lying to you and for...for all the other shit I did. You didn't deserve any of it."

"I didn't," I agreed.

"And I know you'll never forgive me, but for what it's worth. I've grown up a lot. I grew up a lot from losing you. I wanted to come back so many times and beg you to forgive me, but I don't deserve your forgiveness."

"Well, I appreciate it, nonetheless."

"But you don't forgive me..."

"Forgiveness is earned, Nate. You've never done anything to earn it." Ben had. Ben was working every day for it. Doing whatever I demanded.

"Would you be willing to let me try?" He rubbed the back of his neck, a crooked grin on his lips.

Ben and I were separated and working on our issues. It wouldn't be cheating, but I still wasn't sure it was what I wanted.

I swallowed. "What are you proposing?"

"Just one dinner? Even if it's just to catch up...as friends."

"We can go out for brunch tomorrow. It's not a date. I get my son back in the afternoon, and I won't see you while I'm with him. My time spent with him is all his."

He nodded. "Brunch tomorrow is perfect. Thank you. You...look beautiful, by the way."

I flushed red. "Thank you. Now...quit stalking my office building. My employees were ready to barricade the door."

He laughed, giving me a wink as he took a step back. "Whatever you say, boss. See you tomorrow at ten?"

"Tomorrow at nine," I corrected, just to have the upper hand. I was learning that was something I liked.

CHAPTER THIRTY-FIVE

BEN

After my week with Gray, it was time for me to bring him back to Palmer. We alternated weeks with him and spent one day of the weekend together. It was slow and steady...we were in no rush. We were finding our happy medium, and I was gaining her trust back one step at a time. I let her lead the way.

I'd learned from my mistakes and grown into a man I could be proud of, just as she had grown. I was so incredibly proud of all she'd accomplished in the past two years. I wouldn't give up on her or on us. I loved her too much. I wouldn't give up unless Palmer asked me to, and she hadn't. I had gone to therapy monthly, taken her out on dates, taken Gray to Daddy and Me classes, gone back to work. Done whatever she asked to prove to her how much I wanted to change. How much I *had* changed.

I didn't blame her, honestly. If the situation were reversed and her crazy ex took my son, I didn't know if I could've looked in her eyes without feeling disgust, either.

The irony of that thought wasn't lost on me as I

walked up the stairs to her apartment and learned what I was about to. As I reached her door, I found myself staring into a set of familiar eyes. Eyes I'd never forget in a million years.

He turned to me, nodded, but didn't linger. He didn't recognize me. I meant nothing to him, though he took everything from me. I knocked on Palmer's door with a fire in my belly, bile rising in my throat.

"What the hell was Nathan Creswell doing here?" I asked, my body trembling with anger.

"How do you know Nate?" Palmer asked, taking our sleeping son from my arms.

"How do *you* know Nate?"

She flushed red. Before she answered, the realization hit me. No. There was no way *her Nate* was *my Nathan*. "He was...my ex. The one before you."

My stomach dropped. "What are you talking about?"

"Nate and I dated for eight years before you and I got together. How do you know him?" she asked again.

I shook my head, finding it hard to catch my breath. I couldn't tell her. Not now. Maybe not ever. Perhaps therapy wasn't working as well as I thought if I could still lie so easily. "Just from...you know, around."

She gave an unsure laugh. "Okay..."

"What was he doing here?" I pressed. "I thought you hadn't talked to your ex in years."

"I hadn't," she said, her voice guarded. "He came by my office yesterday. Wanted to grab brunch. We just got back."

I kept my face still, emotionless. I couldn't react. To react would be to lose it.

"We're seeing other people, Ben. You agreed."

I did, technically, but just because she pressed the issue. She needed space from me, and I couldn't blame her. "Right, yeah. Of course. I just didn't realize you were seeing him. You said he was an alcoholic. That he cheated on you."

"People change, Ben. I'm not dating him, anyway. We just went out for brunch. As friends."

"Are you planning to see him again?" I clenched my fists at my sides.

"Maybe. We didn't talk about it. Is it a problem?" she asked, walking to lay Gray on the couch. She headed back to me, her arms crossed.

"Not at all. I wish you the best, you know that. But I'm not giving you up." I nodded, hoping I sounded more genuine than I felt.

"I never asked you to," she said, a hint of a smile on her perfect lips. I leaned down to kiss them, just barely.

When we parted, her cheeks had flushed crimson. I still did that to her. "Listen, I've got to go. I have work in an hour."

"Sounds good." She leaned forward, giving me a quick hug and a peck on the cheek. "See you this weekend?"

"See you then," I vowed. By this weekend, all would be well again. By this weekend, Nathan Creswell wouldn't be in my way. I waited until she'd shut the door to dart down the hall and onto the street in time to see which direction he was headed. He stopped at a little red sports car, digging in his pants pocket for his keys. Adrenaline coursed through my body as I approached him.

"Hey, bud, can you help me with something?"

He looked up, his lip curled. "What's that?"

After you'd killed once, it wasn't that hard to kill again.

I wondered if he felt the same. Then again, he wasn't a murderer. Not technically. It was just manslaughter. Wrongful fetal death, they'd called it. A .28 alcohol blood level, a stoplight he couldn't be bothered to stop at, and a car crash that would end the world as I knew it.

"I've got something in my car, but I can't carry it alone. It's for Palmer, the woman upstairs. She didn't want to leave her son alone…"

He groaned, looking up at the apartment building. He didn't want to help me. That was the kind of person he was, but he'd do it for Palmer. He wanted her again. At least for a little while.

"Fine. Sure." He shoved his hands in his pockets. "Where'd you park?"

"Oh, great, thank you so much. I'm just right around here," I told him, pointing around the side of the building, past the security camera's line of vision. I'd never stepped in front of them, keeping a safe space. If anyone watched them, they'd never see who he was talking to. He followed me around the building and toward the back of the parking garage.

"You really parked in a shitty spot to be unloading something," he said, looking behind him at the journey he believed we'd be making.

Oh, how wrong he is.

"I know, man, what can you do? This street is always packed. Everyone's constantly in and out."

"You live here?"

"Not anymore." *But soon.* "This is me." I pointed to my silver Mazda. "It's just in the trunk."

He walked around to the trunk, and I opened my driver's side door, grabbing the tire iron I kept under the seat and popping the trunk. I shut the door, and Nathan opened the trunk. He looked up at me with confusion. "What the h—"

I swung, ending the sentence and, from the amount of blood that spurted from his skull, I'd guess his life. I hit him again, just to be sure. He fell into my arms, and I shoved him in the trunk, groaning and grunting until his weight was off of me. I closed it firmly and wiped away the spattered blood from my face, arms, and the car. I used my shirt to clean the weapon off last, tossing it back onto my floorboard.

I stared in the rearview mirror, adjusting it. I couldn't feel good about what I'd done, but it was what was necessary.

Nathan Creswell had already taken two of the four things that mattered most to me, and I'd be damned if he took the only two that remained.

I said I'd do anything to keep Palmer this time, and I meant it.

Anything.

I pulled out of the parking garage and headed the opposite direction that I'd been intending to. I might be late for work. I needed to make a pit stop in Red River. Thanks to Kat, I knew the perfect place to bury a body.

It was the least I could do for her.

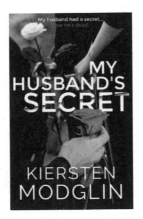

DON'T MISS THE NEXT KIERSTEN MODGLIN RELEASE!

Thank you so much for reading this story. I'd love to invite you to sign up for my mailing list and text alerts so we can be sure you don't miss my next release.

Sign up for my mailing list here:
http://eepurl.com/dhiRRv
Sign up for my text alerts here:
www.kierstenmodglinauthor.com/textalerts.html
OR text KM BOOKS to 31996

ENJOYED THE LIAR'S WIFE?

If you enjoyed this story, please consider leaving me a quick review. It doesn't have to be long—just a few words will do. Who knows? Your review might be the thing that encourages a future reader to take a chance on my work!
To leave a review, please visit:
https://amzn.to/2V5q9Rv

Let everyone know how much you loved
The Liar's Wife on Goodreads:
https://bit.ly/2ClIe77

ACKNOWLEDGMENTS

First and foremost, I have to start by thanking my husband and daughter—I'm so grateful to have you two in my corner, celebrating every success and pushing through every failure. I love you and I could never repay you for all we've made it through together.

To my family—Mom, Dad, Kaitie, Kortnee, Kyleigh, Granny, Papa, Nan, Pop, and so many aunts, uncles, and cousins—thank you for giving me books for almost every holiday or birthday and notebooks for all the rest. I wouldn't be here without you!

To my beta reader, Emerald, thank you for always being the first cheerleader for my stories and for giving me such amazing advice. I couldn't do this without you and it wouldn't be half as fun to try.

To my editor, Sarah West, thank you for always believing in my stories and for pushing me to make them the very best.

To my proofreading team at My Brother's Editor,

thank you for being my final set of eyes and for always finding those pesky typos that manage to sneak through.

To my fans—thank you for believing in me and supporting my dream. Thank you for being readers and supporting art. I'm forever humbled and grateful for all of you.

And finally, to you. Thank you for purchasing this book and reading my story. Whether this is your first of my books or your twentieth, I hope it was everything you expected and still nothing you could've guessed.

ABOUT THE AUTHOR

Kiersten Modglin is an award-winning author of best-selling psychological suspense novels. Kiersten lives in Nashville, Tennessee with her husband, daughter, and their two Boston Terriers: Cedric and Georgie. She is best known for her unpredictable suspense and her readers have dubbed her 'The Queen of Twists.' A Netflix addict, Shonda Rhimes super-fan, psychology fanatic, and *indoor* enthusiast, Kiersten enjoys rainy days spent with her nose in a book.

Sign up for Kiersten's newsletter here:
http://eepurl.com/b3cNFP
Sign up for text alerts from Kiersten here:
www.kierstenmodglinauthor.com/textalerts.html

www.kierstenmodglinauthor.com
www.facebook.com/kierstenmodglinauthor

www.facebook.com/groups/kierstenstwistedreaders
www.twitter.com/kmodglinauthor
www.instagram.com/kierstenmodglinauthor
www.goodreads.com/kierstenmodglinauthor
www.bookbub.com/authors/kiersten-modglin
www.amazon.com/author/kierstenmodglin

ALSO BY KIERSTEN MODGLIN

STANDALONE NOVELS

Becoming Mrs. Abbott

The List

The Missing Piece

Playing Jenna

The Beginning After

The Better Choice

The Good Neighbors

The Lucky Ones

I Said Yes

The Mother-in-Law

The Dream Job

My Husband's Secret

THE MESSES SERIES

The Cleaner (The Messes, #1)

The Healer (The Messes, #2)

The Liar (The Messes, #3)

The Prisoner (The Messes, #4)

NOVELLAS

The Long Route: A Lover's Landing Novella

The Stranger in the Woods: A Crimson Falls Novella

THE LOCKE INDUSTRIES SERIES

The Nanny's Secret